TABLE OF CONTENTS

I will praise You, O Lord, with my whole heart

I will tell of all Your Marvelous works.

I will be glad and rejoice in You;

I will sing praise to Your name, O Most High.

-Psalm 9

BOOK ONE

have something to confess. More and more I find myself talking with people about our Lord. I can't help it. The Good Lord has been so magnificent and generous with me that I feel the need to share how beautiful and wonderful He is. I am not pushy nor do I force my views on anyone. I simply hint at it in conversation and if the person is open then I share my experience. I feel so fortunate that God has been ever present in my life and especially during the tough and dark times. I find that the Spirit is so powerful and to not share it would be a disservice to the people who surround me or whom I encounter in my life journey. God is good. Those of us who have witnessed His power and magnificence almost have an obligation to share that incredible world and news with others.

I am by no means perfect. I have many flaws and work on them to make myself better. That does not mean that I can't share and give testimony to people regarding our Lord. He has performed many miracles in my life and has been my rock and shield through it all. I tell people that I feel like I have won the lottery many times over because of how many blessings God has bestowed upon me. I am no different than anyone else. God loves absolutely everyone with a compassionate heart and He is there for you. He is a forgiving and a loving God. His Infinite Mercy knows no bounds or limits. He offers us everything in this life including eternal life. I also believe that God's times are perfect. Sometimes a person is not ready to receive God and still has to learn many lessons in order to get there. That is okay. He will always be there for you, waiting patiently like a Loving Father.

In my most difficult times I fell into clinical depression. I wanted to take my life and foolishly felt that it was the right thing to do. In those dark times I turned to our Lord. I simply told Him: Lord take the wheel as I can no longer bear this. He did and I was able to lift myself with His help out of that twice in my life. I didn't have any money. I simply stood close to God and He provided everything else. I did a Master's program in psychology where they let me pay as I went along. Unbelievable? Not for God. I could tell you many stories in my life when I was down and out and He came to my rescue. Too many angels? Not for God. In different times in my life he sent many angels to my rescue to provide what was needed at the time. Improbable? Yes, highly improbable and against all odds but that has no bearing on the work of our Lord. So whatever you are going through know that the Lord is there for you, waiting to show you His Love and Compassion. Ready to guide and comfort you. Ready to be your rock. Ready to be your shield and ready to be in your life. I promise you that.

My God is a generous God. He is a giving God and he gives abundantly. His love overflows to every person and to every living thing on earth. I feel very fortunate that I can see how God has guided my life with His loving hand. I tell people that with our thoughts and actions we are always either planting good seed or bad seed. If you do good acts you are planting good seed. All good seed produces good fruit and it always gets paid back. Maybe not today, maybe not tomorrow, but as sure as the sun rises every day the good always gets paid back. If you are smart then you would plant the good seed in large quantities so that you can harvest the good in large quantities. So don't just plant the good seed in your own garden. The fields are vast and there is truly no limit as to how much good seed you can plant. There is also no limit to the abundance of blessings that are waiting for you. Sure, we do not do the good because of the blessings we expect to receive, but believe me they are part of the outcome in doing good deeds. The Good Lord is not stingy. He would like to give you all of the blessings that He has promised and even more. It is all up to you.

My God is an understanding God. I might not have been so understanding and compassionate with myself. He has looked past my weaknesses and given me many, many, chances to redeem myself and help myself to become a better person throughout my life. God is good. I can attest to the fact that even in the worst of times I can see how the Good Lord has been guiding my life and teaching me something that could not be learned otherwise. How to learn humility if it isn't through a life experience, how to learn forgiveness if it isn't learned in the school of life?

These most essential and important lessons cannot be learned in a classroom nor can you learn them from someone else — you have to live them in order to learn them. God has granted me that school of life as well. I am grateful to God for everything. I am eternally in debt to Him for this wonderful life and the many experiences I have lived on my life journey. My God is a protecting God. He takes care of every step in my life and makes sure that I do not falter. Even in the darkest and most remote corners of the world God is there to protect you and deliver you. Even in the worst danger and in the worst situation

God will be there to cover you and will have your safety and well-being. God has your back.

God is magical. I know that this sounds unbelievable and it is. When I speak to people about our Lord sometimes I feel like the Holy Spirit is talking through me. I am not one taken to fantastical realities but I have to share this if I am going to render a true picture of our Lord. On many occasions I have had those whom I am talking to tell me: "Look! Look at my skin I am getting goosebumps just listening to you talk about God." I feel like I am transmitting something that is beyond human but that can cause a physiological reaction in others that is not commonplace. If it were simply an emotion it would be different. But some of the people I have talked to feel my words with their whole being. I have witnessed this many times empirically and that is why I am including it here. God is amazing.

Don't cheat yourself in life by not reaching out to Him. Give Him a try. What do you have to lose? And look at everything you have to gain. He is ready to receive you now even if you do not think you are ready — He will set the table and welcome you in His loving arms. The Lord is my fortress, He is my Savior. Trust in Him. He will protect you every day of your life. Pour your heart out to the Lord. He is ready to listen.

Let me tell you a story. Once, I was on the street with nothing but the clothes on my back. My fiance had kicked me out of our house and I was broken hearted, hungry, emotionally destroyed, exhausted and tired. I didn't have a dime in my pocket and I only had half a bar of charge on my phone. I didn't have anyone to turn to locally because I was not in my home town or state. I called someone who I knew would not lend me money but might find a way to help me out. They did. They were able to purchase a one way ticket back home to South Texas for me with their miles and I would have to pay them back in cash.

The only problem was that the flight was not until the next evening and I did not have a place to stay. I had to find a ride to the airport and maybe I could spend the night there. I called another person to see if they could find someone to give me a ride. They did. A friend of theirs was at a conference in San Francisco and was willing to leave the conference to pick me up in San Carlos and take me to the airport. This angel picked me up and took me to the airport as a favor to my friend. I was incredibly grateful.

I got to the airport but since my flight was not leaving until the next evening they could not let me through security. I asked the person at the security entrance if they could let me by. They pointed me to a Delta agent and told me they could grant me a temporary pass. I didn't even know that this existed or was possible. The agent gave me this yellow slip of paper and they allowed me to enter the security checkpoint.

I went straight to the gate where my flight would take off the next evening and looked around to see how I could get comfortable to spend the next 24 hours there. I was starving. I was waiting at the gate when I saw that there was a flight that evening to Texas which had my same itinerary. I asked the man at the counter if there was any way he could get me on that flight if there were any empty seats that I could fill. He said

"Absolutely! That will be $200". I told him that I did not have a dime and could not afford that to which he said he was sorry.

I waited for everyone to board and then I saw that the man left the counter and another man took his place. Everyone had boarded the plane by now and I thought I would ask again. I did and he told me "Absolutely. The cost is $200". I told him I did not have a dime. Suddenly, I heard the printer underneath the counter starting to print. He handed me a first class ticket and I could not believe it! I gave him thanks, took the ticket, boarded the plane, and proceeded to order a complimentary sandwich and a beer. It was certainly one of the most delicious sandwiches of my life.

So I went from being on the street in Northern California at 7:00 p.m. with no money to being back at home in South Texas and having my mom picking me up at 8:00 a.m. the very next day. This incident always reminds me of a pastor who always used to say: "I am son of the greatest king" because that night I felt the presence of our Lord and his hand in guiding me safely back home.

I tell people that the strength of my faith is based on the many experiences where God has had my back. I can no longer be afraid. I know He is there for me and I know that He is infinitely powerful.

I spent a year back home and after a year I went to St. Jude's shrine and spoke to the Lord again. With all of my heart I prayed to the Good Lord and I said to Him: "Lord, you know my heart and you know that I am here to serve you. If you would like me to serve you here then by all means please keep me here, but if you think that I could serve you better elsewhere then by all means please take me there." Three days passed and then I received a call from a tech company in Silicon Valley. They wanted me and would pay to relocate me and bring me back to the bay.

The Lord will always be with you if you follow Him, Love Him, and follow His Law. He will always guide you and lead you to where you have to be. He will always give you what you need, show you the way and bless you in many other ways. All you have to do is to follow Him, love him and walk in the light. For me His Primary Law is very clear: Love God with all of your strength, heart, mind and soul and Love thy neighbor as Thyself. You have to make God your primary love and follow his commandments. When we help people whether it is feeding a person in need, encouraging someone, uplifting someone or listening to someone who is going through a tough time we are doing the Lord's work. In loving our neighbor we are Loving God. Each one of us possesses a Soul. A spark in our being that is God in us. When you take care of someone else you are honoring not only the love God has for you but also the Love that God has for your neighbor and for every living thing, you are honoring God in us. So you see you do not have to feel alone. You are not alone.

I wish you could have lived my life to see how clearly God has been so present in my life. I am just like you. The only difference might be that at a young age and by what I thought was an accident I ended up on a church trip that changed my life and brought me closer to God. In that trip I learned how to pray and started to discover the magnificent World that God had created for me. For any of us this conversion can happen at any time. We are meant to be born again in this world and to walk in the light with God by our side.

It is easier than you think. Pray to God and build a relationship with Him. If you want to be happy, if you want peace in your heart, if you want a complete life then look for God. He is always ready to receive you. I assure you that you will thank me once you discover how beautiful and abundant that world is. I understand that perhaps right now you are in too much emotional pain, you feel alone and you feel that the whole world is against you. I have felt like that too. You do not have to take on the world by yourself. Choose God and put it all in His hands. I assure you that you will be better off by doing this. He will cover you with His Love and deliver you from any evil that surrounds you. He will lift you to extraordinary heights and show you the way to bliss. He will be your loving companion forever and ever. I promise you that.

To sum up my life, it has been big peaks and valleys. I have reached the highest peaks and also felt and been in the lowest valleys. It is in the lowest valleys that I have learned the most important lessons in life: obedience, forgiveness, faith, humility, and compassion.

I believe that in life we are given to learn life's lessons and until we learn them do we move on to the next lessons that are more advanced. The most difficult ones are the ones that are learned during hardships and in troubled times. The hard times are the ones that also bring us closer to God and allow us to feel the strength of His presence and His power. I have had and lost.

I have had to start over in my life several times and never felt that I could not reach the highest peak again. At one point in my life I was in trouble with the law, I was in debt, I was being sued by multiple parties with different charges both civil and criminal. Yet, I knew that everything was happening for a reason. There were many things that I would learn from all of these very low valley experiences.

As someone has said before — "The journey of a thousand steps begins with one single step." I feel this confidence because I know that God is with me. I know that His power surrounds me and protects me. I have seen it and I have lived it. Countless times have I been in the midst of danger or certain that I will suffer an accident but I have always seen it through unharmed. No matter what fate may befall me I will remain unshaken and trust in my God.

Moreover, and in many parts of my life God is omnipresent. For example, I recently lost a very good job because of a senior executive and I did not doubt that a better opportunity would come to me with the help of God. It did. Actually, two bigger and better opportunities opened up for me. I never cursed the man that manipulated things to push me out of my job. I blessed him and prayed to God for him. I did the same thing with my ex. I forgave her and prayed to God that she would find happiness and comfort in life. I never cursed them. That is not for me to do. I trust in the Good Lord and know that He always works things for the best. The Lord will always see you through. He will always act and although you cannot see the outcome of the acts you will certainly see them in time. Have Faith.

The Lord's power is much, much, much bigger than this world. This world is only a spec on a spec — A dot within a dot. The Lord is as vast and powerful and as ever expanding as the universe. He is not limited by small things or what you might consider large or impossible obstacles. To move a mountain for the Lord is child's play. Trust in Him. He loves you like only a father or mother could love a child. He loves you with a complete and overflowing love. Look, I am not perfect. I continue to make mistakes and leave things that I should do left undone. Sometimes I feel like I am not doing my best and I push myself to do better. It is easy to get stuck and to be lazy and not act. But you have to persevere. To not correct your mistakes is a mistake. You have the whole world in front of you and it is yours to conquer. Go after it knowing that you have the biggest power in the universe at your side. You put in the hard work, be consistent, persevere and The Good Lord will do the rest.

Some people say "I will believe it when I see it". I wish I could show you. I wish you would have lived in my life to see all of the wonderful things I have seen. I wish you could have traveled in my shoes. I can only tell you and hope that you will listen to me. You do not have to be in pain. You do not have to suffer emotionally. Lift yourself up to the Lord. Lift your heart up to the Lord. Give him your sincerity and your troubles. Pray with faith and your life will change.

You see I am no different than you. We are the same. We are all composed of the same materials: matter, energy and spirit. What I have lived you can live too. Break the chains that are binding you down. Break free of the negativity and of the darkness. Begin to live the life that you were meant to live.

Rejoice in the kingdom of God. Take the first steps and do not be afraid. He has you.

I basically tell people the same thing. If you go to the gym every day and you take it on as a discipline and are consistent, what is going to happen? Your muscles will get bigger, you will lose body fat and ultimately your health will improve. This is physical development. If you go and take a lot of classes and are persistent and continue to take classes and read many books throughout your life and you take it on as a discipline every day and are consistent, what is going to happen? Your memory and reasoning will improve. Your deductive and analytic reasoning will get better and you will ultimately improve your thinking and mental faculties. This is mental development. If you go and learn psychology and are persistent and continue to understand this science with resolve and dedication, what is going to happen? You will learn to understand yourself better which can ultimately lead to loving yourself and you will also learn to understand others better which can ultimately lead to empathy and compassion or to loving others. Through psychology you have the potential to achieve a better relationship with yourself and a better relationship with others. This is psychological development and maturity. If you go and take on a spiritual discipline and are persistent and consistent, what is going to happen? Your inner peace will grow, your heart will swell with love, you will learn to let things go and to forgive people, you will learn the value of helping and taking care of others.

The Spirit is man's highest power, his true Hope and Promise. Herein you will find the majesty of life and the richness of God's kingdom. Here you participate with everything that exists in the universe and not only our little tiny world. When you develop your spirit you gain a sense of the wholeness of the Universe, you converse with this beautiful world and ultimately you will commune with our Lord God. This is the perfection of your being. If you develop this there will be nothing that can stop you, there will be peace in your heart, you will gracefully walk to happiness, abundance, and success in life.

As your spirit grows so does your inner peace. When you see and feel this peace grow within you it becomes your immense treasure. You begin to value it and ultimately it becomes your richness, it becomes your irreplaceable gold. You will not want to sacrifice or lose it. You will protect it with everything you have and you will not allow anyone to disrupt that peace. You will only want to grow your inner peace further. It is truly a magnificent and beautiful thing. You are really missing out if you don't even try to work on this part of your being.

My God is a Loving God. His Loving-kindness is infinite. His Love is Vast and never ending. His Love covers and envelopes me. The Lord is my Fortress. He is my shelter. Under his wing I find refuge and protection.

I was telling my brother this morning that the laws of the Universe and the way of the Lord are very simple. In this world there is only light and darkness. In the light you will find love, movement, creativity, compassion, positivity and peace. In the darkness you will find hatred, no movement, destruction, harm, negativity and conflict. The light is of a higher frequency and is not heavy or dull. The darkness is of a lower frequency and is heavy and dull. The light is the good and the dark is the bad. Follow and choose the light and follow the laws of our Lord. Reject the darkness and move away from it. Run the other way when you see the darkness and follow your path of light. The good Lord is light and love. He overflows with light and love for you. The Lord is a Lord of relationship. He gave up and sacrificed his only son, Jesus Christ for our salvation. Giving up your son is no small sacrifice. Yet he did it for us out of His Love for us. Love is the factor that connects us in this ordered universe.

Philosophers, skeptics and scientists please take note. If you emphasize empiricism and experience I asked you to open your eyes wider. It is only possible to prove what you are willing to hear. How is it possible that I can wake up in the middle of the night at 2.37 in the morning out of a deep sleep and instantly think of my best friend whom I love at the precise time that he was having an accident? In the precise moment when he was suffering and had experienced a shock I was awakened and the first thought out of my mind was oh my Lord what has happened to my friend. If you know me then you know that I am the heaviest of sleepers and it is not easy to wake me.

Furthermore, how is it possible that at the precise moment when I am enjoying a truffled pasta in Las Vegas my friend whom I love sends me a picture of the exact same dish that I was having but he was in Italy having that same dish without either of us knowing where we were or what we were doing at that time? How is it possible that when my mother is in trouble or pain she suddenly comes to my mind and something inside me makes me feel a pressing need to call her? The same thing on the inverse. When I am feeling bad perhaps from a fever I hear my phone ring. It's my mom calling asking if I am okay. How does she know in this precise moment that I am not well in health? How is it possible that when old friends that I have not spoken to in years suddenly come to mind so I give them a call and they tell me it is really funny that you are calling because I was just thinking of you? I haven't talked to them in years and they just coincidentally also had the same thought.

Is it just a coincidence? I don't buy that! How is it possible that sometimes when I text my girlfriend we are thinking and texting to each other at the exact same second if we haven't sent a text all day long? Just yesterday, a friend I had not talked to in about 2 years took my call from a new number and said: "I can't believe you just called me. I was literally just outside, smoking a cigarette thinking I need to call Ricardo". If I was to draw up an equation that showed what the odds are of all of these actions taking place in the precise moment that they do it would baffle your mind because it is nearly impossible. What I conclude from everything I have seen and understood is that this universe is an ordered universe and it is bound by love – the Love of our Lord for us and the bonds of love that we have for each other.

The way of the Lord is through relationship, through understanding and through nurturing. We are connected. We belong to each other and should cherish and love each other. We spend too much time judging each other when instead we should be helping and loving each other. You don't necessarily need money to help another person. By simply listening to someone who is going through a difficult time you are helping them heal. By giving a word of consolation or an uplifting thought you can help a person. By feeding a person with the food that you have you can help a person. By volunteering with causes that help people you are doing your part.

I find it incredible that we have the power to change a complete life around. We have the power to uplift a human soul to change through love and inspiration. It doesn't always happen but it is always a possibility. I find it amazing that we have the power to change a life. You never know with the good seed you plant if your words will inspire or motivate a person to change. Maybe it's a word of understanding or knowledge that you share with a person that produces that moment when they realize that there might be some truth to what you are saying. Maybe its just the feeling of love that they feel coming from you. Whatever it may be I find it to be incredibly powerful that a whole life can change with simply conversing with someone.

Moreover, there are many ways to help and they are all truly fulfilling. We search for fulfillment in life and most of us search for money or material possessions only to find out that is not true fulfillment or true enrichment. God teaches us with the example of love and compassion that is embodied in the life of Jesus Christ. I assure you that all of the pain and loneliness you are feeling right now will be different if you follow the ways of our Lord. All you have to do is make the choice to walk in the light. Confess your sins to our Lord. Speak to him. Pour your heart out to Him. He is patiently waiting for you. Tell him your deepest secrets. Hold nothing back. Serve your life up to him, repent. Promise to walk in the light and serve Him and others. I guarantee that your life will change.

My Lord, my soul thirsts for you. Like the arid earth thirsts for moisture my soul and body wait for you. I am here to serve you my Lord please send me as many as I can help and console with my words, thoughts and actions. For I am here to do your work O Lord, to follow your law, to walk in your light and to sing praises to your Glory and Name. Lord, I meditate and pray to you with all of my heart. I thank you for all of my blessings and am grateful for this joyful life which you provide. Help my brothers in their time of need. Shine your light in their path. I love you Lord, my strength, my rock. You light my lamp and turn my darkness into light.

Lord, I am grateful for all of the blessings that you bestow upon me. I thank you for having a roof over my head, a bed to sleep in, a heater to keep me warm, and for the food that you graciously provide for my nourishment. I thank you for my loving family and my loving friends. Dear God, I bless you and thank you for my life, for my sustenance, for my health and for my well-being. Lord, I thank thee for everything.

Lord, make me strong. You are my redeemer, my hope and my promise. Although I continue to fail in many things and fall to temptation repeatedly you continue to extend your boundless love, understanding and forgiveness to me. Thank you Father. Thank you Lord.

Dear Lord, although I can see darkness quickly approaching on the horizon my faith in you in unshakeable. My resolve is stronger than ever. I stand here knowing that if it is your will then it shall be done. My love and faith for you are steadfast. I stand here unafraid. Whatever storms, sickness or pestilence I should have to weather I will weather. Whatever darkness is to come my lamp is shining brighter than ever. Your Will be done. Whatever I must face I will lean on you. Not as I will, but as you will. You are my shield, my redeemer, my rock and my fortress. You are my everything.

I tell people the same thing. What I believe in is real. Just like you believe that this chair is real and you would be willing to bet all of your hard earned money and are certain that it is real, I also believe that my God is real. I don't believe in something invisible. My God is more real and more visible to me than anything in the world. This is because in the hardest parts of my life He has been there for me. He has sustained me and lifted me up in my most difficult times so the Lord is more real than any material thing in this world or than any person or friend in this world. He was my friend who was there when I needed him the most. He was there when no one wants to be around you or associate with you because of your broken condition or poverty. He was there: to console me, to love me, to listen to me and to uplift me to unbelievable heights. He is my best friend and my father. He has been there even when I didn't ask for Him and sorely needed help. So how could I not believe in Him?

He who was there during the most critical times in my life. He who loves me with an unbounded, steadfast and infinite love. He who forgives me for all of my weaknesses and trespasses. I am of all sinners one of the worst because I clearly understand right from wrong and yet I fall to temptation very often. He has always been there for me and if you open the door He will always be there for you.

18

"Ask and it will be given to you; seek and you will find; knock and it will be opened for you. For everyone who asks receives, and the one who seeks finds, and to the one who knocks it will be opened."

-Matthew 7:7

So again, you are never alone. Don't ever feel alone because you are not. You are not the first or the last person to feel like this. Even though the pain is so strong that you think that no one has ever experienced this believe me many people feel that same pain. I know that sometimes it can feel unbearable. Never give up. Millions of us have been there. It is very important that you understand that you are not alone. God is always there for you.

Once you find God you will not imagine how you lived without Him in your life all of these years. Once you find Him you will want to share the good news with everyone. You will want to share His greatness with every person you meet. You will feel like if you don't share your experiences you are doing a disservice to humanity. Perhaps at this very moment you cannot see it. When we are in our most difficult moments we cannot imagine that even this difficulty will also pass. There is not a storm, no matter how bad, that will last forever. We live through good times and bad, through moments of joy and suffering. Yes, life includes suffering but suffering does not last forever. You have it in your power to overcome it. This too shall pass.

So in my mind I have been asking myself: How do I pay it back? How do I show God how grateful I am for all of his love, understanding, and compassion towards me. How do I show

Him my appreciation for all of the blessings that He has bestowed upon me and all of the blessings that he continues to give me? I have been reading the Holy Bible for the past couple of years trying to figure this out. I think God wants us to love him just like He loves us: Unconditionally. I think God wants us to put Him first when we are thinking of our decisions and of our acts. He wants us to follow His law which is very clear from the commandments. Furthermore, I can show him my appreciation by following his law and walking in the light. Also, I can tell people about his glory and share my experiences with others. I can help spread goodness in this world. I can always be open to smile at people, to help spread joy in the world and to fill others with hope as well. I can be someone who will listen to those who are in sorrow or who simply need someone to listen to them. I can uplift and inspire those who need inspiration or feel like they are in a rut in their lives. I can also take some of my blessings and help feed people and support them especially those who are most in need. I can volunteer to charitable organizations and help a lending hand in every way possible. I can also serve my family and help them in every way I can. I can help mentor the youth and guide them in their life journey to find success and happiness.

But I think the real question is what would happen if many of us did this. What would happen if hundreds or thousands of additional people would set out to do the good in our communities? Many people are doing it today but what would happen if we could get many more to add to that. What if we could change the hearts of many people to do the good instead of the bad? What if we share the message of God everywhere.

Wouldn't we be better off in our communities? Wouldn't we create a better and safer world? Lord, isn't this what you would like to see. Lord, hear our prayer.

Some people like to ask: what is the meaning of life? I would say that the meaning of life is to find joy, peace and happiness in your life. So how do you find that? I would say that the first step is to find God. Commune with our Lord and learn about his ways. Develop your spirit in many ways for that is your strongest power. For some people meditation, contemplation, prayer and yoga will help them develop the spirit and grow their inner peace. For some the way is through the heart and they will find their happiness by serving and giving to others. Still for some it will be letting go and releasing their attachment to material things or possessions. For others it will be letting go of greed, envy and malice and doing the good instead and understanding that at bottom our life is more important than any material possession which can only bring a semblance of temporary happiness. In some cases for others it will be releasing resentments held against others and learning to forgive. For others it will be realizing the importance of loving yourself and loving others by understanding and having compassion for them.

Life is precious and it passes by very quickly. We must learn to prioritize what is most important in life which is love. Don't overthink it. We are very good at making excuses for ourselves and being in denial about what is truly important. We need to look in the mirror and say I want the best life for myself and my family. Live your best life.

I believe that we are born in this life materially to find out that we have to be reborn in this life spiritually. We are born as a seed with all of the potential to become a large and robust oak tree. Yet many of us do not find our way. We are called to grow and to develop in this life to the best of our potential through the development of our being. We should work on developing ourselves physically, mentally, psychologically and spiritually. Furthermore, we are called to love one another and not just this person and not that person but to love everyone.

To forgive those who have acted against us does not mean to permit them to do it again. We also need to love ourselves and not allow them to hurt us. In forgiving others we bless them and continue on our own path. Can you imagine if we become examples of God in our lives and serve as a beacon of light and hope for others? We can be that light that shines bright for others to see.

When you meet a spiritually developed person you can see it in his eyes. You can see a profound peace in their eyes which is reflective of the development of their spirit within. I have met many remarkable people like this. They are a fine example of what we are ideally called to do in this life. It is blessed to live with an inner peace that you protect and harness. This does not mean that you will feel and act like a superior to others. Quite the contrary. If you are developed spiritually you also understand that you are first a student and you are here to serve. Part of this spiritual development also includes understanding humility and the truth that we are all the same, that we all have an incredible potential, that we are all children of the same God. True, we may all be different in many ways but essentially we are all the same. We all have the same capacity to grow and develop and I would say that that is what we are called to do. So, again, what is the meaning of life? That's easy: to become the best you, to become a living example of God's love for you and God's love for all of us. Each path for us will be different and highly individualized but they are all leading to the same place.

Dear Lord, thank you for giving me so much. Thank you for giving me the gift of life. Thank you for upholding me and for giving me your infinite love every day. Thank you for always guiding me and showing me the right way. Thank you for enlightening me and for teaching me the ways of life. Thank you for your infinite grace, thank you for your mercy, and for your understanding. I am forever in your debt and grateful for everything that you give me. Although at times I have questioned and doubted you, and at times I am negative in many ways and make bad decisions and feel depressed... thank you for always standing by me.

I think I know how you feel. You feel alone and misunderstood. You feel like no one can understand your pain. I assure you that many have felt the same way you are feeling right now and that many are feeling that way right now as well. I assure you that in the future more people will also feel the pain that you are feeling. The struggle, the fight, the surrender and the suffering are all part of life. You feel like you have no energy and you feel empty. You are feeling isolated and alone. You are in a dark part of your life and you need to move past that.

I always tell people the same thing. You need to move. Motion and activity are the opposite of what you are feeling. Start exercising and moving around. Start moving and stay active. Be productive and see if you start to feel better. Pick up a sport or start running on a daily basis. The best way to get out of the rut you are in is to start by doing the opposite of what you are currently doing. You don't have to be sad and gloomy.

The first steps are always the hardest. Once you get moving you will see that it is not as difficult as it looks. Keep fighting. Your happiness and the love for yourself are right around the corner. Appreciate who you are. Talk to God. He is waiting for you to reach out to Him. You don't need to make the transformation by yourself. God is there to help you. Break the negative thought patterns. They will get you nowhere but only to destruction, only to hurt yourself. Remember: In this life you are either being creative or destructive. Choose the light, choose happiness and choose to create a better life for yourself. I love you. Time to get some rest now.

If you have some time I can tell you my story. My name is Ricardo. I was born in May of 1972 in a small southern town in Texas of about 40 thousand people known as Mcallen. I was a sick child growing up and had to battle asthma in my early years. This sickness always kept me very close to my mother as she would always take very careful and loving care of me. My first birthday was at a nightclub. My grandparents owned nightclubs for 46 years so throughout my childhood I was always around and working in nightclubs.

My family was lax Catholic so we would not go to mass regularly and only for social events like first communions. One day, at a very early age maybe about 8 years old while attending mass I felt something overpowering. I felt something so strong and so emotional in the middle of my chest that I would never forget that moment and feeling for the rest of my life. It was a very strong feeling of love and joy and it was unmistakable. I believe that this was the first time that I felt the love of God and the Holy Spirit. I would describe this feeling as my first calling to serve our Lord, my first conversion.

After that I lived my life like a regular shy and insecure kid. I took my first job at the age of 13 working for my grandparents in the nightclubs. I learned some of the most important skills and lessons in life like having a strong work ethic, loving my work and taking pride in everything I worked on. I have found some of these lessons to be invaluable now that I look back upon how much they have helped me throughout my life. My grandparents always gave me a lot of love and were very patient and understanding with me. They taught me many things all of which I am very grateful for.

At the age of 15 my best friend invited me to go to Rome and told me that his father was going on a business trip and we could tag along. He was lying. The trip was a Church trip and they were going to Yugoslavia to see the apparitions of the Virgin Mary in Medjugorje. I was a very late addition and the Church had trouble in allowing me to go as I was already known as somewhat of a partier. This trip changed my life. I believe that this was my second calling, my second conversion to serve the Lord.

In this trip I met a very skeptical kid that was my age and we had very long debates about the existence of God and what everything meant. We concluded at the end of our long discussion that we both wanted to give our lives to God and decided to go to confession perhaps for the first time bearing everything we could think of and leaving nothing unconfessed. At the moment that we decided to do this we were in a small café and a very large storm hit the village. We did not think that we would be able to find a priest in the middle of the night and much less in the middle of a large storm. We did. There was one lone priest sitting in a corner withstanding the rain and we had the honor of confessing our sins to him. I would tell you of many miraculous things that I witnessed in this trip but maybe we can save that for another time. Suffice to say that this trip was where I learned how to pray with all of my heart and were my life direction would become clear.

After this trip it was not difficult to chose to attend a private Catholic liberal arts school which would give me my formation in philosophy and my absolute love and passion for education. The quest for Truth would turn out to be something that was taken very seriously in my life and I would fight hard and persevere in my studies toward that end. This heroes journey of the quest for truth would mark and direct me for the rest of my life.

In the summer after finishing my first year of college I had the opportunity to travel to the South of Spain to a town called Marbella as an English teacher for Catholic children. I loved the experience so much that I decided to stay in Europe and attend my second year of college in Rome. My University had a small campus that was 30 minutes south of Rome and I was more than excited to attend for a semester.

From there, I was able to travel all around Europe and I loved it so much that I decided to find a program where I could continue to study philosophy and still be able to explore Europe. I thought that the best approach if I was truly searching for the Truth was to attend the most prestigious and secular University in Spain. I did. I was accepted and challenged at this institution and it proved invaluable in understanding and defending what I believed in with all of my heart.

These two years in Europe truly changed my life and perspective. I began to understand that because I had been in a certain culture and was taught to believe and do things in a certain way it did not mean that there were not other valid ways to see and live life. It opened me up to many different ways of thinking and made me consider life and culture in different ways. I went back to finish my university studies and ended up with the equivalent of about 7 years of education as I was always taking the inter-term classes and winter classes when other students were at summer or winter breaks back at home. I studied political philosophy, natural philosophy and Spanish American literature. I was a b student for most of my classes with the exception of the subject of philosophy which is still to this day one of my strongest passions.

I went back home to prepare for the Lsat as I thought in the back of my mind that is how I would find success. Thank the Good Lord that I did not follow that path. I did ok on the test and was even admitted to a law school but in the end I chose to go back to the nightclubs and work for my grandparents.

Soon after that at the age of 22 I opened up my first business which was an upscale bar and grill with Mexican food and a very busy bar that was opened very late into the night. I did somewhat well in this business which allowed me to open my second business this time a Martini Bar in the north of Mexico. I was also somewhat successful with this business and proceeded to open a nightclub in Mcallen and then another in San Antonio. I felt at this point like I was on top of the world because of the material success I had attained but also deep inside I realized that I was truly alone, sad and miserable. This part of my life, although it was a lot of fun, was also my saddest.

I isolated myself from my family and true friends and became a Narcissist. So many people telling me that I was so great affected me and led me to believe that I was some kind of amazing person. I was wrong. One fine day I lost all of the businesses, my material possessions and everything I believed I was. This was when I suffered my first clinical depression.

I had gotten myself into an enormous amount of debt and was even in trouble with the law. I was also being sued by some greedy people who thought they could gain by hurting me. This was the darkest period in my life. I tried to take my life and spent countless hours considering how to do it. I realized at one point that I had learned and done so much in my life that the best thing to do was to turn to God. I had abandoned my faith and God for many years now and it was time to turn back. I talked to God and asked him to lead me wherever he wanted me to serve Him. I turned my life over to Him and asked Him to do His will.

After that, I was accepted into a Masters program in Psychodynamic Psychotherapy. I knew I wanted to at least help people and Psychology seemed to be the best tool in order to accomplish that goal and also would be part of my pursuit of truth. I didn't have any money. The school allowed me to pay as I went along and even let me keep some of the small fees that we charged in order to get by. I find this part of my life to also be miraculous. At this point in my life this marks my third calling or conversion. I truly had no idea what I was going to do with my life or how I was going to get out of the mess I had created for myself and God provided me with this amazing and life changing opportunity.

I had to travel twice a week on a 4 hour bus ride each way to get to the school but none of that mattered. I was determined as ever to get back on track and succeed. This education truly changed my life. I literally sat in class open mouthed and could not believe how much truth there was in all of these behavioral patterns, defense mechanisms, and personality disorders. As I was studying this program and also helping people by giving therapy I was also studying the East. I had spent a good part of my life studying the West at the College level that I realized that in order to have a full picture I really needed to study the East. I began to study Buddhism and to practice meditation. I became a master in several Buddhist disciplines and began to study Hinduism as well.

After the program ended I decided to Move to New York as my sister had offered me to be her roommate. I happily accepted this invitation and felt that if I could make it in New York then I could really make it anywhere. I started working odd jobs as a server, host, and manager in restaurants and had the time of my life. I was even the Russian outside the Russian Tea Room in New York and I was responsible for dressing up with the Russian Coat, top hat, and everything. I felt like I was the authority on 56th avenue as I had a whistle and would illegally direct traffic to hail customers a taxi sometimes.

I was avidly reading many Hindu texts as I fell in absolute love with Swami Rama, Yogananda, Vivekananda, Aurobindo and all of the Hindu Masters. I could not believe their teachings. If what they were teaching was true and we had known this for over 4 thousand years then why weren't we following what we knew to be true and beneficial to man? I had to find out. I took on a meditation discipline that had me meditating every morning. I learned as many methods of meditation and immersed myself in all of the teachings of these Hindu Masters.

As fate would have it, after 4 years in New York my sister had to move to northern California. She offered for me to move with her to which I had no problem in accepting that invitation. Once in Foster City, California it was time to find a job so I started to look for one. When I first opened Craigslist I could hardly believe that there was a position as a part time administrator at an Indian Company known as Kerala Ayurveda Academy. Their offices were located less than a mile from where I was living at the time. I could not believe it. I put on a suit and went to interview for the position. They accepted me and I started working for them right away. This part time admin position became a full time position and I quickly became their director of marketing and sales. Not only had I found a great job but I was learning so much from the Ayurvedic Doctors that taught not only medicine but also Hindu Philosophy.

All of this training and learning led me to a deeper conviction and love of my Faith. All of this preparation served to get me closer to God and to appreciate His Love. I was able to feel the depth and beauty that we have as human beings even though I understood that I was just barely scratching the surface. This training also helped me understand that there are many paths to God and any one of them is as valid as the next.

Moreover, I then met a girl through Facebook and we began talking and fell madly and passionately in love. We decided to move in together and became engaged to be married. After the third year of being engaged I started freelancing my marketing skills so my income became reduced by about 40 percent as I had to work small jobs for different clients in multiple industries. I think that at this point she began to lose respect for me because I could not afford the lifestyle we had been accustomed to. One fine day, I came home to find out that I was no longer welcome there. She kicked me out of our house and this marks the second time when I hit rock bottom.

I fell into clinical depression again and decided to move back home to South Texas to spend one year living close to my family. After this year I went to St. Jude's Shrine and spoke to God once again. I prayed to him with all of my heart and I reiterated to Him that I was here to serve Him. If He felt that I could serve Him better where I was then He should keep me there but if He felt that I could serve Him better somewhere else then I asked Him to please take me wherever that place might be.

Exactly three days passed and I got a phone call from an important Tech Company in Palo Alto. They wanted me to come work in their office and they would pay me to relocate and help me in finding an apartment. I could not believe it! I moved back to the Bay Area and after being at this job for a couple of weeks I was contacted by a recruiter. He told me I would be perfect for this position he had with a consumer goods company in a beautiful setting in the heart of the Bio Tech Park in South San Francisco. I told him that I could not take that job. I had a responsibility and a commitment to the Tech company that had been generous enough to bring me back to the Bay. He insisted and insisted so much that I got tired of him calling me. I told him that if he re-wrote my resume and got me the interview I would go but I would not accept the position under any circumstances. After I attended the interview I met with the owners of the company and they offered me a position as a marketing director making a lot more than what I was making and also added many benefits to the package. I took the job. Once I talked to the tech company they were eager for me to continue to work for them and allowed me to work remotely. The Lord had now blessed me not only with one incredible position but even against all of my resistance had given me two positions and two incomes. I felt so blessed. The Lord had always taken care of me and now He was raising me to a height professionally that I would have never thought possible.

I am so grateful for all of the opportunities and doors that the Lord has opened up for me that I decided to study in earnest to try to understand what God wanted me to do. This I believe was my fourth calling or conversion. At this point God had done so many things for me and answered me so many times that in my mind the thought that God exists was irrefutable. Now I wanted to show my appreciation to God my father and God who was undoubtedly my best friend and my everything. I felt like it was time to pay it back. In other words, how could I pay God back for all of his blessings, for all of his protection, for lifting me up beyond all of what I imagined was possible.

I had previously studied the Bible in college and throughout my life but this time I was going to go deeper to try to see if I could understand how to show God my appreciation for everything. In my study so far I have deduced that perhaps what God calls us to can be summed up in one of the books of the gospels. At one point the Pharisee which was the expert of laws asked Jesus mocking Him: Teacher, tell us, what is your supreme law? What is the law by which all of the other laws fall? What is the main teaching and the key to your kingdom? And Jesus answers him: "Love God with all of your heart mind and soul and Love thy neighbor as you would thyself". The Golden Rule seems simple enough. When we read it we say well of course, I love God and I love others. But the deeper we analyze the Supreme Law the more we begin to understand that it means a lot more.

The first point is that you need to Love God and only God. You can not have another God. For many of us our God is Money. Money determines how we act or react to many things.

We cannot worship the golden Calf if we want to participate in God's Kingdom. We need to truly love only God and follow his law which is not always easy to do.

For example, if someone wrongs or hurts you your reaction should not be to hit back. That is not what God teaches us. Clearly, you should not allow yourself to continue to be hurt so you should take yourself away from that person who hurt you. Loving yourself is also part of what God wants for you and in loving yourself the last thing you want is to allow anyone to hurt you. You should forgive this person. That is not easy to do. You have to put your ego and pride aside and truly forgive the person who hurt you and even pray for them. God instructs us to love everyone even our worst enemy. You have to leave what this person did to you in God's hands. He will take care of giving each his due. What is more important is your own peace and your own freedom.

If you bear a resentment for that person who hurt you the only thing you do is hurt yourself. Holding on to grudges and resentments is like holding on to a hot coal which is damaging and burning your hand. In the same way emotionally if you are holding on to hatred you are hurting yourself. Don't do it.

I have never wished bad things on those who have hurt me or tried to hurt me throughout my life. I feel like I have been naturally gifted with detachment so for me it has been easy to forget when others have wronged me. Just yesterday I heard from someone who had confabulated and orchestrated wrong against me. He was suffering and hurt from something similar to what he had tried to do to me. I had not heard his name in many years and even when I had it was just in passing. Now here it was on a social media post on how he was angry and in pain regarding something of the same nature that he had tried to do to me. I did not feel happy that this happened to him. I felt bad for him. Even further, I felt like he could have learned this lesson in private and not allow himself to be publicly humiliated. I felt really bad for him. On the other hand, I did feel like it validated what I have come to understand over the years: everything eventually gets paid back. You see, I didn't have to do anything. I never had to fight that war. I didn't have to react and try to hurt him in a similar way in which he tried to hurt me or in some other way. Everything always balances out. Leave it in God's hands.

Now let's go back to the law. How else do we show or exemplify the ardent love that we have for God. Certainly by thanking him in prayer and expressing your gratitude by thinking about our Lord and his law throughout your day. We can also show him our love by reading the bible and contemplating and meditating on his law. Also, we can walk according to his teachings in our life. Being the light can have a tremendous effect in our lives and also in our society. This is how we can Honor God.

How else can we serve our Lord? Having Faith. In the gospels, Jesus repeats over and over about the importance of having faith in Him. Have Faith in the Lord and put all of your trust in Him. Also, helping our neighbor and especially those which are in most need. If we follow the example of Jesus in the Gospels this teaching is very clear. Jesus spends his time healing and helping others. We need to do the same. We need to bring love, compassion and understanding to others especially those who are most in need. Every time we have someone come into our life who we can help is a big opportunity for us. That is how I see it. If we are able to help them we will be planting the good seed and increasing our treasure in heaven. The more we can help others and do the good deed the more we increase our own true worth. Also, it is sometimes tricky because our ego and vanity speak to us and make us think that we are exceptional human beings. We are not, at least not in the sense that our ego would like us to think of ourselves. We are working on it and the sooner you can forget the good deed you have done and move on to the next one the better.

I always tell people the same thing. True enrichment is comprised of those things that no one can take away from you. This enrichment is yours and you carry it with you everywhere you go. For example, in spiritual development you grow your inner peace and it become bigger as you persevere and practice. No one can take this inner peace away from you. It is yours. You have developed it. The same goes for life experiences. These are yours. No one can take them away from you. The same goes for your mental capacities you have developed and grown these. No one can take them away. This is true enrichment.

Now on the other hand, material enrichment which is what we typically consider enrichment is different. You can wake up the next day and all of that money can be completely gone. This is not true enrichment. You can lose it in the blink of an eye. Some misfortune can come into your life and you have to spend everything you have been so diligently working to accumulate. So my advice is to spend some time enriching and growing yourself with true and lasting enrichment and the things that truly matter like love. Devote yourself to developing and growing yourself. I always tell people that we are born like a big block of stone for the artist who is a sculptor. We have a choice to remain like an undeveloped block of stone. If we take our calling seriously we can develop ourselves into a perfect sculpture of a human being. We just need to chisel that block of stone. We need to persist in making ourselves better and chiseling our lives to reach our true potential. It takes a lot of work and persistence. It is not easy. But like everything, if we take it one step at a time and are constant we will surprise ourselves with what we are able to accomplish. Remember once you develop into a perfect Bernini sculpture no one can take that away from you. You have grown and developed into this beautiful being.

If there is a blueprint for happiness I would speculate based on my experience that it would have to include loving god, loving and helping others, being close to God and developing yourself physically, mentally, psychologically and spiritually. The physical is important because without health you cannot do anything. Health is wealth. It would also have to include doing what you love. Many of us have to go through jobs that make us unhappy. I believe that life is too short to be unhappy. Sometimes we have to put up with what our bosses put us through but you are also free to seek other opportunities and to find a place where you can be truly happy. I know that it is not easy but not trying and not acting in pursuit of your happiness is also something you should avoid. Remember not acting is also a choice.

At this point I would like to stop and thank you for listening to me. I can go on and on if you do not stop me and we could be here for days. So thank you for the bottom of my heart because I whole heartedly believe that some of what I have been telling you can help you. I only wish that I could change the way you see yourself but only you can do that. You are an amazing and uniquely beautiful human being. You are capable of many extraordinary things and hold a unique gift in your talents that you can bring to this world. You are a magnificent soul capable of seeing, feeling, hearing, sensing, experiencing, breathing, and loving. You are a gift from God. There is not another person in the world like you. You are a masterpiece of systems working together, regulating each other and working in perfect harmony. Your life is precious and it is remarkably yours to choose what is best for you. At all times you are making choices. You have that power to make a choice and choose a different path in your life. It is all up to you. I can talk to you about which path to take but ultimately it is your own decision. I am only sharing my experience because I think that you are cheating yourself out of this wonderful and exceptional world if you do not at least consider God. Look I can tell you many stories, believe me I still have many, many more to tell you. But what would that accomplish?

I am not trying to convince you. I am simply stating that to me it is undeniable that God exists and that He loves you deeply. So how many stories of the miracles I have witnessed would it take to make you believe? Maybe I need to explain myself further. Do you have time? I just want to continue to share my perspective.

To me it is very difficult to say that God does not exist. To say that would mean that I would have to negate or deny every time the Good Lord has taken care of me, watched my steps, and kept me away from harm and trouble. To negate God I would have to ignore my whole life. I would have to say that the many many times that my friends and I drove severely intoxicated on our many trips across the border to Mexico to get drunk were extremely lucky as we never suffered any harm. From 14 years of age to my early thirties I was a partying disaster. My family owned the nightclubs and I threw the parties at said clubs. At a very young age of about 16 our parties were what you would consider wild. We threw all you could drink parties and the club was opened all night long into the morning hours. We were the very definition of partiers sometimes having over a thousand people in the club from the surrounding high schools who would come out to Mexico for the bars, restaurants, nightclubs and for the parties. We had a ton of fun. My life for this time period was extremely fast. During the summer we would spend 4-5 days out of the week going to different restaurants and bars in Mexico and partying hard. How we all made it in one piece and unharmed when we were completely irresponsible is still puzzling to me just based on the sheer number of visits and the excessive amount of alcohol that was consumed. We held all types of parties. We would have all you can drink Everclear parties in South Texas as well.

I would also throw formal dinner parties in Mexico at my grandparent's house with my closest friends and sometimes even their parents. After college, the same thing ensued when I owned my nightclubs. Nights were filled with parties at the clubs and also in homes. I was not into hard drugs. I had seen from an early age of working at the clubs how dangerous and destructive drugs could be so I was scared for the most part of consuming them. I remember clearly how I had gone out with two really attractive girls that were avid customers of our club and much older than me once. They really scared me out of the hard drugs as they were regular users and were a complete mess.

So with all of these nights and all of these crazy times, I never got hurt. I was able to come out of it in one piece and that in itself is truly miraculous. I think if you did the math on all of the possible times that I could have gotten hurt and was kept away from danger, you would be astounded too. Thank you, God.

Also, there is the time when I was standing outside one of my nightclubs like I did ordinarily. It was early in the evening and I was used to always stand outside while my workers were getting everything ready for the evening. I would stand in front of the club and talk to my security guards before we would start to get busy. One night I was doing my typical routine when a waitress came and let me know that a vip table was requesting that I join them at their table for a toast of something they were celebrating. This was very odd as I had never truly had a request like that. They were asking me to join them for a glass of champagne. I obliged. Once I sat down to share a glass of champagne with them we heard gunshots go off outside. Two of my security guards who where standing outside had been shot. That would have been me. There was a young customer of ours whom they had been having fights with and he came to shoot them and the club up. It was shocking to say the least. It took me a long time to recover and to finally be able to go back to work at the club again. I know you saved me that night lord. I know it in my heart. I was just there seconds before he came to shoot up the club. Once again, thank you Lord.

Then there is the time when a jealous and crazy boyfriend almost slit my throat for going out with his ex-girlfriend. I was completely intoxicated but I remember feeling absolutely no fear when he put the large blade next to my neck. I saw the hatred and anger in his eyes. I still to this day remember his chilling words telling me that in that moment he could take and end my life. Literally sobriety washed over my whole body from head to toe. I answered him that the only one losing would be him as my life would be ended and he would have to deal with the consequences. He ran away. He was a customer and brother to a very good friend so I felt completely safe inviting him to the house and having drinks with him, that night we were sampling tequilas and cognacs. I had no idea of what his intentions where because I had honestly not really cared for his ex. I just went out to dinner with her once and I really didn't like her to begin with. But he was crazy about her. So crazy that he had planned to put that blade on my neck and maybe in a moment possibly kill me. I didn't react or make any sudden moves or show any fear. Thank you Lord for saving me that night.

What about that time on New Year's Eve in Mexico City. I was at a party with my girlfriend in a relatively bad part of town. I only went there because my aunt was dating this guy and we were going over to his apartment to celebrate new years eve. After my girlfriend left I was still at the party and then very late into the morning hours I just went outside and started walking. I was completely intoxicated and did not know this at the time but walked into perhaps one of the worst neighborhoods in Mexico City with a tux on. I sat down with some guys that were hanging outside of their home and we got to talking. I was sharing my life with them and I think they just could not believe that I was there because they probably knew the type of danger I was in. One of the guys confronted me and asked me if I knew what it was like to be hungry. I told him I did but probably in a very different way than he had experienced it. I was very fortunate to not get killed or beat up that early morning as well. Thank you Lord.

I could go on and on with stories in my life where God clearly saved me from harm. I don't know why. I just know that he has done it many, many times for me. He has always kept me away from danger. How could I not be grateful? Not only has the Lord completely blessed me with this life, with all that I have experienced, given me in abundance of things but also he has always kept me from danger. The Lord has also always had my back and fought my battles. I know its hard for people to understand but for me it is very clear. I have seen people try to wrong me throughout my life and those people have usually gotten their due. I didn't have to lift a finger. Whether it was God or the Universe that took care of things one thing is certain: I never had to fight those battles.

I understand that two wrongs don't make a right. I understand that you should never retaliate from a wrong. I just know it in my heart. God's path is through the light not through the darkness. God's path is in kindness not in hatred. You should love your enemy and all people for that matter. That is your acceptance of God's covenant with mankind. God knows you by name. He knows you and he has plans for you. All you have to do is believe, follow his commandments, and love Him. The Lord promises us Eternal life in return. Isn't that amazing? It is not a small thing he is promising us - it is eternal life.

So you see for me I see things very clearly. I see what I have to do and although I have the understanding, I still fail miserably at so many things. I am still a big work in progress. I still fall to temptation. Yet, even despite all of my shortcomings, all of the times that I have forsaken our Lord He still forgives me. He still loves me, He still guides me and He still watches over me. He Loves with a love that is deeper than a mother's or a father's love. He loves completely and without restraint. His love is steadfast and abundant.

So to summarize, I would tell you that to me it is inconceivable to think that God does not exist. God has had a very clear presence and place in my life and to deny him would be to deny my very existence and life. It makes me feel very sad when I hear that someone does not believe in God because I can only think of how empty and lifeless that life would be. It is also pretty hard to believe that I tried to take my life during very difficult times because I love and appreciate my life so much now. I guess what I am telling you is that the world of hurt, emptiness, darkness and pain that you are experiencing right now is the opposite of what the Lord has in store for you. When people deny God It makes me sad because I feel like denying God is like cheating yourself out of the beauty and incredible wonder which is this Universe and this world. I wish more people would give God a try. After all, what do you have to lose? And you have a whole Kingdom and even eternal life to gain. I would say that it is something very much worth your time. In my heart, I would love nothing more than to tell and share with everyone about the good news! To share the gospel. To share the majesty and absolute perfection which is our Lord. To share the ever flowing life which is our Lord. The unconditional love with which He loves. Like a father who waits up for his prodigal son to return ever patiently and with a heart full of understanding, mercy and forgiveness. I can only share my perspective and life experience, the rest is up to you. I am here to support and help you in any way I can. Repent, for the kingdom of God is upon us. We are out of time for today but I thank you very much for listening to me. Please know that I am always here for you.

Dear Lord, now more than ever we need you. We pray to you and we ask you for forgiveness. Lord, please forgive us our sins. You know my heart. We are all selfish liars and self interested for our own gain. I am very quickly seduced to pleasure, impulse and to wrong doing. Our world continues to show disrespect for human life and dignity. There is much hatred in the world but there is also a lot of love in our world. We only hear about the negative things but in this world there are more good people than there are bad people. It only seems like a dark world because you only hear about the bad people and bad acts. There is still no excuse about how we are treating our world and environment and of the violent atrocities that we are committing in this modern world. We can change, and we can be better. Please forgive us.

Moreover, I would never hurt anyone and even think twice to kill a bug. I can't even punch a person and never have. I have learned forgiveness and have never truly had a problem with that. I even embrace my enemies although I have to admit it has been difficult at times. I love my neighbor with all of my heart although I catch myself often thinking otherwise. I truly honor and care for my mother and my father for they are both very special to me. Although like everyone else my life is full of white and noble lies that at their root are not evil. What I have not done is where many of my faults are also. I have not given enough or helped enough as I have in my heart to do. Everyone I encounter as you know I try to share your glory but I have not extended my charity to others in need. I will work on this. I promise you. Please forgive me for ignoring or not thinking about you for so many years of my young and adult life. It has taken me time to get closer to you but I have failed you in many ways. I am sorry. There have been many times when I have not loved you with all my heart, mind and soul. I am sorry for that as well. I like many of my fellow brothers and sisters have worshipped at the feet of the golden calf. I am sorry. As you know, I am also a work in progress in humility. I have not come even close to perfecting that. Furthermore, I have failed to keep the sabbath holy many many times. I have worshipped pleasure for many years of my life where I gave no opportunity to worship you or even consider you. I have never truly coveted or wished what my neighbor had and if I did briefly, I never dwelled on it. I know that many are called and few are chosen and I know that I am far from you considering choosing me as I know I have many shortcomings. I will continue to study your law and meditate on what you want from your servant. I will do better. I am very grateful for all of the blessings that you continue to bestow upon me and I will be a better steward of these gifts. I promise you that.

Today, I share my life story with whoever is willing to listen. I use Lyft to commute to work every weekday and I always engage my drivers. Sometimes I share parts of my story, sometimes I only share the main points and sometimes I don't have the opportunity to share anything at all. I am an open book. When I share my story with people many of them also open up about their thoughts and about what they think about what I have learned. I find people fascinating. Every person is a complete world of thoughts, impressions, opinions and perspectives. I learn a lot from people and I do it because I genuinely want to help and I am also trained to help them or at least to give a word of encouragement. I feel like sometimes God sends me people that need my help. Being a passenger with Lyft over the years has allowed me to meet many people from very diverse backgrounds whom I have shared my life and perspective with to the best of my ability. Dear Lord, thank you for providing me the opportunity to share my testimony with these people. It is a tremendous honor to be able to sing praises to Your name.

Sing to the LORD, praise his name;

proclaim his salvation day after day.

Declare his glory among the nations,

his marvelous deeds among all peoples.

For great is the LORD and most worthy of praise;

he is to be feared above all gods.

-Psalm 96

BOOK TWO

"Because he holds fast to me in Love, I will deliver him. I will protect him, because he knows my name. When he calls to me, I will answer him. I will be with him in trouble. I will rescue him and honor him. With long life I will satisfy him and show him my salvation."

Psalm 91

have to admit it. It is time for me to come clean. I am going to tell you the whole truth. I am a Miracle of God. I am only here in front of you because of God. My Lord and Savior, The Lord Jesus Christ has made all of this possible. He has protected and rescued me. He has hidden me when I have been in danger. He has been with me and by my side this whole time and especially during my toughest days. He has always delivered me and answered me, even if it was not the answer that I wanted to hear at the time. He has always been there for me. That is the truth. He was there for me when I was in deep trouble. Like a loving Father, He has always covered me with His love, mercy and understanding. He has rescued me from certain ruin and destruction many, many times. He has embraced me and has shown me His wisdom. He has guided me in my life and has shown me right from wrong. His law is perfect and simple.

With his ever-shining and eternal light He lights my path. I am forever grateful to Him. With His steadfast loving Heart, he has shown me His compassion. He has cured my sicknesses. He refreshes my soul. He has always cared for me. Thank you, my Lord.

Someone asked me the other day how I built up my faith. I told him that for me it was simple. God was there when I was down and out. He was there during the most difficult and most vulnerable moments in my life. He was there when no one else wanted to be. He was there when people were avoiding me because they thought that somehow my bad fortune might be contagious and affect them by associating with me. My God has been there for me. Always. So you see, for me, life is one big miracle. How God came to me during my most dangerous moments and saved me in the nick of time is still miraculous to me. He saved me even when time had run out. In the last fraction of a second, He came to my rescue. And not only has He done that but He has done that many times for me throughout my life. So how could I not be grateful to God? How could I not make him my A Number One? How to reject a beautiful faith that has made it possible for me to be telling you this story. The Lord has done so much for me. Believe me, I gave him more than a thousand reasons to leave me, and He didn't. He never gave up on me. Moreover, He continues to bless me abundantly. He nourishes me and rejuvenates me. He is my Lord and Savior. My God in Whom I trust.

My faith is heartfelt and built up on a rock. Every large concrete brick represents the gratitude I feel for what the Lord has done for me in every instance. They are held together by the Love that I feel for our Lord. This fortress was built over time as I grew in faith and in proximity to our Lord Jesus Christ. You can do this too. All you have to do is start.

I think you would agree with me if you heard my life story. You would most certainly have to conclude that God is with me and has always cared for me. From being saved from an angry mob in high school to getting away in the last second from a car jacking in Dallas to being rescued in the last moment from a gang beating me up, you would have to conclude that the Lord has always protected me, He has always sent his angels to guard and save me. Any of these instances could have gone horribly wrong. They could have quite easily been the end of me. But I am here.

The other day a driver asked me if my faith was based on my intuition. I explained to this person that my faith is based not only on my intuition but also on my complete life experience. My faith is based on what I have witnessed here in this life. It is based on me putting everything together in my life, of measuring it and submitting it to critical analytical reasoning. I actually feel like my faith has grown as I review and contemplate many things, events and occurrences in my life that I tend to forget, as we all do. As I review my past, I realize that the Lord was and is always there for me. He was always there to pick me up, to lift my head, to console me and to be my redeemer. So you see? How could I ignore the single most important anchor in my life. How could I possibly stand by and listen to someone say that He doesn't exist. That is so antithetical to who I am and to everything that I have experienced in my 50 years of life. My faith is based on who I am and what I have become thanks to God. It is based on what I have experienced and understand. My faith is in my heart where I hold fast to the Lord. I am grateful for everything the Lord has done for me and for his Infinite mercy. He is my Lord and Savior. He is my redeemer and my guardian.

Maybe you would find it more miraculous if I told you about being unemployed and depressed in a small town in Mexico and how I went from there to being an executive in Silicon Valley with a corner office and an incredible view of the bay. Or perhaps you would be more convinced if I shared with you that I was able to beat depression twice in my life. I can assure you that both times it was all God's grace and love that was able to lift me out of those dark times in my life. It was all God. I only held on tight to His right hand and He did the rest.

Or maybe you would be more easily convinced if you met my friend. He was in a truly dark place battling drug addiction, broke, unemployed and in trouble. He prayed and believed. He turned toward the Lord and the Lord lifted him up out of all of that darkness. He is now happily married and living a healthy and prosperous life. If you want to meet him, I can arrange it. He can tell you himself about how the Lord showed him His love, mercy, and compassion.

The most astonishing thing is that our Lord never leaves us. He is always ready to listen, always ready to welcome us into his loving arms. No matter where you are, no matter how dark, The Lord will come and lift you up and show you His compassion and steadfast love. He will save you.

Or maybe you want to hear about my other friend. She was told by her doctors that she would not walk again and would not be able to have children. Today, she has 2 children and is not only able to walk but runs without any problem. The Lord performed many miracles for her. Our God is a God of miracles. I would like to introduce you to her and you can ask her yourself. She will tell you her miraculous story although I am sure you have heard about these stories before from people you know. It is all true. There is nothing impossible for our Lord and Savior. As we are reminded in the Bible:

Jesus looked at them and said, With man this is impossible, but with God all things are possible.

So you see, the strength of my faith is not only based on the over two dozen times that God has saved and protected me from certain destruction. It is based on everything in my life. From when God first impacted me with an overwhelming burst of joy that I felt tremendously in my chest, to when God first opened my eyes to His Kingdom and I was truly born again in Yugoslavia, to today when I read the Bible and get closer to Him and come closer to understanding His love for me. My faith is based on the most trying and pivotal times in my life. The ones you remember the most because they are engrained in your memory forever. The moments you never forget. The key moments in your life that really could have gone completely wrong. God was there for me in my most needful times. I fell in Love with God because He loved me even when I couldn't love myself. He was there. He showed me His love and He performed many miracles for me, even if I was undeserving. He is my best friend, my companion, my father, my light, my everything.

Just this past Tuesday a couple of houses down from where I live a neighbor's trailer caught fire in his driveway. Pretty much all of it burned to pieces with the exception of five large propane tanks that did not ignite. Do you believe in miracles? I have a couple of stories to share with you.

I am grateful that you are here. I understand that you are going through a tough time and suffering through depression and I truly appreciate that you are here. I am both humbled and honored that you have decided to come. I know that you might feel like you have no energy or desire to move or go anywhere. I know that you feel alone and that no one understands the pain that you are feeling. I sincerely hope that my story and advice will help you in your journey and that you can see the tremendous value that there is in a relationship with God. The Lord has always protected and provided for me throughout my life even in times when I was far away from Him. He will do the same for you. He will lift you out of your current state.

I am also going to recommend some additional things. You need to move. Motion is the opposite of stagnation. Depression is non-movement, dullness, heaviness and sluggishness. We need to do the opposite. Do you like to exercise? How about taking up a new sport? I myself love to walk at a quick pace. I put on the music on my headphones and just go. If I think about it I just might not do it but if I do it without thinking about it, I am already on my way. I also like to pace. I like to move. Do you enjoy dancing? Dance and Music are your friends. On some days, I put on my music when I get home from work and dance around as I clean my apartment. The key is to always keep moving especially when you are feeling bad or depressed. Motion belongs in the category of creativity, love and light. Stagnation belongs in the category of destruction, hatred, and darkness. Walk in the light and avoid darkness at all costs. Run away from the darkness and move toward the light. Do you like to write? Have you ever kept a journal? This is also a good way to get all your thoughts out and not pent up. It can also help you see how you evolve in your healing.

We are also going to work on avoiding all of the negative and destructive thoughts that depression causes. We are going to eventually replace them with thoughts that are positive and creative. Affirmative thoughts and feelings are where we are headed. I am going to recommend that you spend some time reading the Word of God which is found in the Holy Bible. We will begin with the Gospels. You need to study the Bible and I am also going to recommend that you memorize your favorite selected verses. Further, I am going to recommend prayer and also give you some of my go to prayers. All of these actions are actions in the light. They are precisely the opposite of darkness and will eventually help eradicate darkness from your life. I will give you all the tools you need. All you have to do is try it, put some effort in and begin to welcome God into your life. I assure you it is much, much better than your current darkness. You will eventually find peace, love and happiness.

Please promise me one thing: That you will not give up. That you will Never quit. No matter how hard, painful and difficult a day may be please press forward remembering that there is always a next day. Things will get better. I promise. No storm lasts forever and this one will not either. You will suffer wounds which will heal with time and they will be an essential part of who you become. This is part of life. The wounds will be healed and you might even use them to help heal others with your experience and testimony. Just remember it is important to persevere. Never lose Hope. Trust in the Lord and Believe. God will take care of the rest. Also, remember that I am always here for you. I am one phone call away. You are never alone. God is always with us.

EARLY YEARS
0-14

Here is my story:

I am Ricardo. I was born and raised in the small town of Mcallen, Texas along the US-Mexico border. From an early age I was brought up with a tremendous amount of care. I suffered from chronic asthma in my first 7 years of life so I received an enormous amount of attention, devotion and tenderness from my family. Both sets of grandparents showered me with affection. My grandma on my mom's side used to sing softly to put me to sleep. She gently outpoured love to me as she carried me and sang lullabies about God's protection to put me to bed. One of her favorite songs was the one that had me save one of the two apples I received to keep as a gift for God. I still remember that.

My mom took care of me with complete and utter devotion and love. I remember one rainy and very cold evening that I was suffering through an asthma attack where my mom wrapped me up in a thick San Marcos blanket and rushed me to the doctor's clinic so he could administer a shot to heal me. She always had the vaporizer running in my room and I remember that the walls were always sweating water. She would rub Vick's Vaporub on my body and always protected me from even the slightest wind. She cared for me with boundless care, devotion and dedication. My inhalers and devices were ready to go at a moment's notice.

We carried them everywhere. I recall the dry powdered inhalers that required you to put a pill inside of them. It reminded me of my own condition because it wheezed as it spun the pill to release all of the medicine, just like my lungs that would make a similar wheezing noise when I was having trouble breathing. On some nights, I went to bed not sure if I was going to make it through the night.

In my early childhood my mom and I were always very close both physically and emotionally. I was always by her side and she was always taking care of me. I would always cling to her leg and held on tightly. Wherever she would go she would take me with her. We shared a symbiotic relationship and the thought of being separated from her always terrified me. I remember how difficult the first day of Pre-Kinder was for me as I had to separate from my mom. I cried and screamed and was devastated at the separation but it was necessary. During these difficult times I was always sucking on my thumb until that was prohibited and then I supplemented this action with sucking on both sides of my collar. This must have looked hilarious on a daily basis as my collars were always wet and thoroughly wrinkled when she picked me up from school.

My grandpa on my dad's side also showered me with love. We were best friends and I would go with him to work every day I felt healthy enough to do so. He was always remodeling the nightclub so we were constantly doing construction and designing new things. He remodeled the nightclub at least twice a year so we had a lot of research to do along with the design and construction work. I would always hold his hand everywhere we went. One of our favorite pastimes was to go to the paper store to buy Gabriel Garcia Marquez novels that we would collect, read and also give away as gifts to friends who came over to the house. I always felt like a celebrity when I was with my grandpa because it would literally take us over half an hour to get to the store since he would be shaking hands and catching up with all kinds of people we met on the street. It was like he knew the whole town and they all truly respected and loved him, they were always happy to see him and kept him in high esteem. We traveled together a lot for fun and would always look for the best corners in the hotel rooms so that we could do our yoga headstands for five minutes when we arrived to the room. It was one of our things.

My grandma on my dad's side was also very close to me and cared for me with a tremendous amount of unconditional love and selfless devotion. We were best friends. She never judged me and always took my side. I was the middle child and from early on I was the favorite because my brother was more independent. We would always watch all of the popular soap operas at the appointed time. We would eat pan dulce and drink chocolate milk together while we watched our shows. We were super into them. We spent a lot of time discussing what we thought would happen to certain characters and why. She would always take care of me, protected me and even had a room in her house designated as my room. She would take great care in making sure I always had the best outfits, toys, and clothing. After the first seven years of my life, we were inseparable. I started working with her at the register in the nightclub at age 13 and we were incredibly close. We would share everything and she would always give me an immense amount of love, care and attention. I would tell her everything and she also confided in me. We were besties and were partners in everything. She always defended me. She would always advocate for me. We were more than best friends.

So how could someone like me who had received so much genuine and steadfast love come to suffer from clinical depression twice in their life? I was truly filled with boundless care and genuine attention my whole life from many different people. How could I come close to taking my life on these two occasions? The short answer is that depression is a downward spiral and does not care who you are or how much love you have in your heart. It will strike you regardless of your success, strength, stability or notoriety. Clinical depression is terrible, lethal, and destructive. I can tell you how I beat it. It was only through the help of God.

The Good Lord held my hand and guided me through understanding depression until I was able to overcome it. He held me close and didn't let me go. He provided everything and set the scene. He filled me with hope and saw me through these toughest of times. He lifted me up and filled me with understanding to get through it all. My Lord and Savior the Lord Jesus Christ is compassionate and he heals the broken. My Lord is understanding, patient and filled with true and enduring love. He is the hope of the broken hearted and he is the solace of those who feel alone. You are never alone. The Lord will be with you every step of the way. The Good Lord is the defender and redeemer of the broken hearted. As our Holy Bible says:

The Lord is a stronghold for the oppressed
A stronghold in times of trouble
And those who know your name, put their trust in you
For you, O Lord, have not forsaken those who seek you
Psalm 9

Do not be afraid to reach out to God. Do not listen to those destructive and dark voices in your mind. Move forward in light with the Lord. Walk away from darkness. He is your father and is waiting for you to cover you with his loving embrace and protect you. He will heal you and see you through. I want to share my story with you so that you can see how the Lord always protected, prepared and delivered me throughout my life.

God came into my life at an early age. I was about 7 or 8 years old when I felt something overwhelming at mass. We were lax Catholics and would only attend church for baptisms, first communions and sporadically on Sundays. I will never forget that day at Mass. I felt an energy surge that began at my feet and came out through my chest of an overpowering and overwhelming joy. It was so powerful. There was no mistaking what had just happened because it was very emotional. I wanted to know what I was feeling and experiencing. That moment would mark the beginning of my quest in search of the Miraculous for the rest of my life. I had never felt like that before. What was this? It was emotional and unmistakable. I would find out much later in my life that I had been touched by The Holy Spirit in that moment. It would formally mark the start of my spiritual journey.

LATER YEARS
14-21

At the age of 14 my best friend invited me to go with him and his dad to Rome. He told me his dad was going on business but that we could tag along and shop and party in Rome. We really liked The Smiths so we were jazzed at the opportunity to buy all of their records and posters that were not available in the US. I quickly found out that in fact my friend was going to Rome with his dad but that the trip was a pilgrimage to see our Lady of Medjugorje in Yugoslavia. She had been appearing to a group of local kids and there were thousands of devotees visiting from all over the world. The pilgrimage was through Our Lady of Sorrows Parish and I would have to get approval from them to go. My friend and I asked if there was any way I could join the trip which was already full. They thought about it. It took them a couple of days to make a decision because I think they were weighing whether it was a good idea to allow me to go. I had already started getting a reputation for being a partier because I was throwing parties and also because my family owned the biggest nightclub in town. They allowed it.

I would have to book a different itinerary to get there since they were full but they allowed me to join the group. My grandparents offered to pay for my trip when I asked them. They were always very vocal and adamant about how important it was to travel and experience the world and other cultures. They always taught me that in order to grow and mature I would have to go out and see the world where people might not think the same way I did. I would begin my trip through a different route than the group. I would first fly to New York City and from there I would fly to Europe and then to Yugoslavia. In New York, I would meet another teenager my age who was joining the trip last minute like me and then we would travel together.

When I met this kid at JFK I was immediately impressed. He was super smart and very sharp. He was a skeptic and had very strong rational arguments against the existence of God. From the very first moment we began to discuss and debate. I would pour all of my experience and thoughts into this discussion that literally lasted from when we met at the New York airport all the way to Medjugorje. Non Stop. It was a heartfelt and sincere conversation that explored all points relating to God. We would end up at a Café in Medjugorje still discussing all of these points until we reached a conclusion. We both agreed that God was real or at least that there was a really good probability that He did exist. We also both agreed that we wanted to be born again. That we wanted to offer up our lives to the Lord and repent. We decided that we wanted to confess our sins and completely come clean to God. We resolved that we would go to confession with a priest and make our intentions known.

At this moment when we were sitting outside of the Café a huge gust of wind and storm brought heavy rains and powerful winds. It also got extremely cold. We had heard that there were priests that would sit outside of the main church where you could go to confession. However, we realized that it was late into the night, it was freezing and with the heavy rain there would probably not be any priests outside of the church. We went anyway. In a remote corner of the area where confessions took place there was a young lone priest sitting in a small stool shaking from the cold weather. We went and confessed our sins to him in repentance and offered our souls up to the Lord. After confession, the weather cleared up a bit although there was still some light rain. We were elated. We wanted to go up to Mount Krizevak (Mountain of the Cross) to celebrate our conversion. We had heard that there were pilgrims that would go up to the very top where there was a big cross and spend the night up there singing songs and praying to our Lord.

We proceeded to head toward the mountain when we saw one of the most beautiful sights that my eyes have ever seen in my whole life. A beautiful veiled Lady with a very serene expression and a loving smile was crossing our path. She had what looked like a huge white light and glow around her and resembled the images that we had seen of our Lady of Medjugorje. I asked her which way we should go to travel up the mountain since we were looking for the path up to the top of Mount Krizevak. She answered that each one of our paths should be highly individual and that we should each look for our own path up there. After we passed her we both looked at each other and we did not have to say anything. We both knew what we had just witnessed. We proceeded to split up and go up the mountain individually. The way up was difficult for me because it was very dark and muddy. As I climbed, I could not help but feel that this was part of my penance for all of my past. When we made it to the top I saw my friend up there and we were both overwhelmed with joy. We spent the night praying and singing hymns with others to our Lord. This experience is one of the most beautiful experiences in my whole entire life. That night the sky would clear up to bring us a plethora of shooting and falling stars. It was like the universe was also celebrating our conversions.

If you have never experienced the peace of Christ, which is the peace that surpasses all understanding, You should. Go to one of the many sacred places where you can feel and sense the peace and presence of our Lord. I can give you a few suggestions. Fatima in Portugal for one, or Lourdes in France is another. I personally love Saint Jude's shrine in Pharr, Texas. As soon as I get to the parking lot I feel the peace of our Lord which is astonishing and amazing.

The Yugoslavia trip taught me so much including how to pray the rosary with all of my heart and gave me my direction for many years to come. My decision to attend a private Catholic liberal arts school was very much influenced by this experience. I wanted to dig deeper. I wanted to know more about our Lord. Deep inside although I did not know it at the time, I was already on the quest for wisdom, the quest for truth.

My passion and love for learning began somewhat formally at the age of 15. I was a sophomore at Mcallen Memorial High School and it was in my English class that the spark was ignited. I was a c minus student, English was not my first language and I had what was becoming a very busy party agenda to keep me very distracted. However, even with all of this, my English teacher Mrs. Mohill transmitted her love and passion for literature to me. She inspired me and made To Kill a

Mockingbird come to life for me. I was deeply concerned with Boo Radley. What was to become of him? Why wouldn't they just leave him alone? Mrs. Mohill transformed literature into an immense open door that led into all of these new worlds and from that moment I could not get enough of it. She then introduced Dickens and Great Expectations. I became enthralled and completely identified with Pip because I was Pip! I had great expectations and my grandparents were my benefactors. From that moment on, I wanted nothing more than to become a gentleman. I wanted to become a learned gentleman so bad that it occupied my thoughts day and night after I read that book. I was completely immersed in these stories. I fell in love with all of it including the idea of a romantic love, like the one Pip had for Estella. I can say that this class began what would become a life long love for learning and reading. I was never the best reader. For most of my life I had to read and go back and reread paragraphs. I didn't score very high on the SAT reading comprehension part. I struggled with that but I made up for that deficiency by working hard at becoming a better reader through practice.

I started reading all kinds of books just like scout and with her same arduous determination. From classics to trashy novels, I read everything I could get my hands on. I was immersed in all of these worlds full of very interesting characters and stories and my appetite for more grew. I was simply amazed. I would read complete series like Flowers in the Attic and could not help but empathize with these kids. I was deeply awakened with these narratives and extraordinary tales and they would certainly influence and change my life. Make no mistake about it. Reading will change you. Reading books will improve your memory, your attention span and ability to focus, your vocabulary which will also improve your ability to communicate, it will improve your knowledge, it reduces stress and helps you to exercise your imagination. Reading is powerful and can strengthen your mind. If the brain was a muscle reading would be the exercise you would do to strengthen that muscle. Don't overlook it.

And then there was Mrs. Mottsinger. My English teacher senior year of high school. Mrs. Mottsinger was simply brilliant. She was intelligent, witty, sharp, and hilarious. She engaged her students through the poetic words of Shelley, Wordsworth, Lord Byron and Elizabeth Barret Browning. She recited poetry in class and you could tell she was completely immersed in the art and beauty of the content. She felt every single word. You could not help but be captivated by these very special moments. I will treasure them for the rest of my life. Although by this time I had a very demanding social and party agenda I would always try to attend her class. She inspired my love and appreciation for poetry that would eventually mature into the writing of my very own poems. I will always be grateful for these very special teachers that played a key role in my awakening, growth, and development.

High School did not go without plenty of incidents. I want to tell you this story to further illustrate to you how God has always protected and delivered me out of trouble. Even at this time when I was very distracted and not very spiritual, the Lord saved me. Our group of friends belonged somewhere in the middle between nerds and popular kids, but more than anything we were partiers. One fine day our group decided that we wanted to eat outside by the auditorium. We began to eat outside because we enjoyed sitting by the auditorium and some of us were in drama so we felt like it was our place to sit out there and enjoy lunch outside under the shade of the building.

One day a gang member threw a small half pint of milk at us. The carton container hit the auditorium wall and drenched one of our friends in cold milk. We did not think that this was right so we walked over to where the kid threw the milk at us. One of our friends walked up to him and said: Hey man, I don't think it's cool that you threw that milk at us. This smaller guy backed up a bit and I grabbed him by his shirt to push him against the wall to ask him: Hey, who threw the milk? After that we all dispersed and we went inside to finish our lunch. It only took a couple of hours for the rumor to spread that there had been a big confrontation between preps and gang members. This was going to be a war. The kid who threw the milk had a cousin that belonged to the Kicker gang which was the predominant gang at school. The school football team was going to support us and have our backs. They were going to skip practice the next day to confront the gang during our lunch and tell them to leave us alone. That is what happened.

On the next day, about thirty of us went over to confront the group and not to fight them but to put them on notice that we were not going to be pushed around. When we got outside some of them started to move away from the spot and ultimately vacated it completely. Apparently, nothing had happened. The kid that had thrown the milk ran away and there was no major fight that day. The football players all went back to practice and we felt vindicated. Until the next day.

On the very next day we thought it would be prudent to have our lunch in the new cafeteria and avoid conflict by eating indoors. We didn't have the football team to protect us and only two or three of us knew how to throw a punch so we decided to stay inside. Suddenly, a large crowd started to form outside the new cafeteria and we could see them through the glass doors. They started marching in to the new cafeteria and surrounded the whole inside of the building. Then another row of gang members started marching in and did the same thing. Now we were surrounded by lines of gang members two or three people deep inside the building. I was looking at the doors and saw that the kid we had the altercation with had just walked into the building and had three people with him. They were looking for us.

At this point my girlfriend grabbed me by the arm and was pulling me hard to leave the scene. I saw the danger but felt like if I left, I would be forsaking my friends. Next, around five to six police cars pulled up to the building and things started to get very restless. I suddenly felt someone grab me and take me out of the building along with three of my friends. The four vice principals of the school had jumped in and grabbed us to hide us in different corners of the school campus. One of us was in the art department at the northern most corner of the school, another was in the nurses' office in the back room under lock and key, another had been hid in the portables outside, and they had put me in the detention center. What ensued was a full blown riot led by a large mob of gang members from our city and surrounding cities. Kids started throwing food in the new cafeteria, there were people running on top of tables and the gang members started pushing and hitting people. It was pandemonium. I was watching the melee from the detention room as my friend was hearing them try to break down the door in the nurses' office. I asked a kid who was in the detention room with me what was going on. He said that the preps had crossed the line and it was time for payback.

Eventually the police and principals settled down the riot. I would miss the next few weeks of school until things calmed down. The Lord saved me that day from this angry mob and their gang members. He also rescued me the next year in a different misunderstanding that had eight of them surround me outside of school. One of them had crutches so he had given one crutch to his friend and kept another to himself to hit me. Literally, in the nick of time, my friend Branton Box who was much bigger than me, saw what was happening, rushed in, dispersed the circle surrounding me and told me to leave. He stayed calming them down and avoided them hurting or injuring me. I only got one punch in the mouth. The Lord also saved me that day by sending my friend to intercede for me. More than likely that incident itself might have put me in the hospital. So you see, I have a lot to be grateful for to our Lord. He has always kept, rescued, and protected me.

I can tell you many more stories of when the Lord saved and protected me in my life. Would that help you with your faith? Would that help you believe? Why don't you try it? You have a whole world to gain and nothing to lose. The Lord is patiently waiting for you. Like a loving father. He has plans to lead you to prosperity, peace, and happiness.

For me, the Lord has always guided my path from the very beginning. My university studies were not the exception. When I arrived at the University of Dallas as a prospective student I could hardly believe what I was seeing and hearing. Here was a Catholic Liberal Arts University where you were taught by a very talented faculty comprised mainly of what can be described as intellectual giants. The school itself was surrounded and imbedded with thinkers and philosophers! Close by to campus you had the Cistercians, Franciscans and Dominicans, there was a prep school nearby and also a seminary. The faculty itself was comprised of brilliant minds and world renown talent who were passionate about teaching. As I heard about the pursuit of truth, knowing thyself and the importance of virtue I was extremely interested. What were the origins of our Western Civilization and what did they have to teach us? On top of that, the school was a small private school which made the class sizes small and the education more personal. I was completely sold. This was definitely my school.

I enrolled and will never forget the first day of class in Literary Traditions. We received our first assignment which was to write an essay on Homer's Iliad. As soon as I stepped out of class on Friday I started reading and studying in preparation for this assignment. I got right to work. I spent the rest of the day reading and rereading the text and also read supplemental texts to enhance my understanding of the subject matter in order to write a better paper. I wrote what I felt would be something that would be read out loud in class as an example to other students and was certain that my essay would receive an A and perhaps maybe also publication. I thought it was an exceptional paper after I was done with it. That is how proud I was of my finished work. We turned in the assignment on Monday and on Wednesday I received my essay back from our professor. It was a D- with a note that encouraged me to visit the writing lab on a permanent basis or at least for the first year of College. I was undeterred. I was so determined to succeed that I did not even blink. I knew that it would be a challenge but I was not afraid to put in the time and effort to overcome this obstacle.

Soon after that, The Lord blessed me by bringing my dear friend Alvarito Suarez into my life. Alvarito was a short and scrawny Spanish kid with a big nose who was always quick with a joke. We instantly hit it off when I met him and he would introduce me to some of the most remarkable intellectuals in my life through Opus Dei. We became friends and one day he invited some of us for a home cooked dinner and philosophical discussion at the Opus Dei house. I can only say that everyone that I have met in my life from Opus Dei has surprised me with their kindness, warmth, generosity and understanding. I might not be so forgiving with me at that age. The dinner was amazing and we would be invited a couple of times after that as well. For us, this was a huge treat because of our typical college diet was pizza and ramen which we ate on most nights especially the late night ones. We had incredible discussions after dinner that typically involved Plato, Aristotle, and Aquinas. This was incredibly valuable to me because I was learning this in class and also in the dormitories with discussions that went well into the night. I was incredibly grateful for the invitations, dinners and candid conversations.

One day, the group invited four of us to teach in the beaches of Marbella located in the South of Spain. This would take place in the summer, and we would be teaching children in an Opus Dei center and they would pay for our flights, room and board, and would also pay us a generous salary for our work. I could not believe it! All of us took them up on their generous offer and traveled over to this beautiful center that was located on top of a large mountain with breathtaking views. This would mark my next journey into Europe and we took advantage of every part that we could. My good friend and I realized after a couple of weeks that our money was worth exponentially more if we went to nearby Morrocco for the weekend. We did.

We traveled south and found the monumental Rock of Gibraltar and crossed over to Tangiers by ferry. It was spectacular. Once there, we explored the city and made new friends. We spent time in our Djellabas and since our money was worth so much we would treat local friends to breakfast or lunch all the time. We felt like the kings of Tangiers. One fateful day, as we were looking out on the docks seeing the new tourists descend on Tangiers we noticed two very beautiful women who looked to be American. We approached them and guided them through the multiple men who act as tour guides but then demand payment. These guys are sometimes relentless and they will follow you around until you pay them regardless of them doing any service for you. We got them through without being harassed by these individuals and guided them to the actual tourist office in town for which they were very grateful to us.

The next day I was at a local tea shop enjoying the delicious fragrance of mint in the air along with my tea which always had these large deep green mint leaves at the bottom of the glass cups. I was outside of the shop when I noticed once of the "tour guides" start to approach me yelling at me calling me a "Thief" and spitting at me. He was very angry. He was livid that we had perhaps taken some business away from him and confronted me with a very large and shining sharp knife while moving closer to me. The good Lord has always protected me in every instance. Somehow, in the nick of time I remembered I read somewhere that when in danger in a foreign country you can make a scene and scream to attract attention to yourself and perhaps this can help alleviate the situation. I did that. I took my backpack and threw it at him and started to yell and scream off the top of my lungs. It worked. The tour guide was startled and I disappeared into the tea shoppe which had plenty of people to hide myself in. Very soon after that a policemen showed up on the scene and started to question him. I am telling you this story because I want to make it clear that the Lord has always watched out for me. He has always saved me from trouble and certain harm. On this occasion the Lord hid me and did not allow my enemy to hurt me. Thank you, Lord.

I would stay another year or so in Europe and then return to the United States to finish my degree in Political Philosophy. Once I was back, I realized that my perspective had changed a bit. I felt like I understood myself a little better and was now a little more open minded. Experiencing Europe had left me with many beautiful experiences and a realization that people live and think very differently from us but it doesn't mean that they are wrong and we are right. They are just different ways of life. Different ways of perceiving and also living life. In Europe the emphasis was more on enjoying life and less on work whereas for us the importance was more on industry and producing rather than focusing on enjoying our life.

Once I was back to school it was back to studying and learning. I was in Irving and would frequent Dallas in my leisure time. One day a friend of mine and I went shopping in downtown Dallas and found ourselves at a stoplight with no cars around us in sight. I would soon experience something I will never forget in my life. It was one of those moments that are very shocking and so our organism slows down every moment into a very slow motion. I remember it like it was yesterday. Out of the corner of my eye I saw two individuals walking fast towards our car. As I looked to the other side I saw the same thing. Two other individuals were quickly approaching the right side of the vehicle as well. I reacted and saw my hand drop down in slow motion to press the lock button for the doors with my hand. In a question of milliseconds my hand had beaten the people that were coming to carjack us. It was a split second. However, the locking mechanism had locked our doors and when the carjacker pulled on the door handle he found it locked. I felt an overwhelming chill that traversed my body and down my spine from my head to my toes. The carjacker looked at me and smiled revealing a complete set of gold teeth in his mouth. I slammed on the gas and peeled out of there as soon as possible even though I was at a red light. These moments always stand out for me because

I know it was moments when God had my back and saved me. The Lord has always watched out for me even in the days when I was far away from Him. For all these moments and so much more I am eternally grateful to our Lord.

LATER, LATER YEARS
21-and on

I graduated and then decided to go back to work with my grandparents at the nightclubs. I worked for a couple of years and then opened my own in Laredo, Texas. I was somewhat successful with these businesses so I opened another one in Reynosa, then another in Mcallen, and finally one in San Antonio. I considered at that point that I was successful but one fine day it all came crashing down and I had to sell what I had left over to pay debts and get out of legal trouble.

This would mark the most difficult time in my life so far. This was my darkest season. I lost everything and fell into a clinical depression. In life you will have all types of seasons some bright and some dark. You will have highs and lows. You will have seasons of incredible joy and abundance and you might also experience seasons of sadness, darkness and scarcity. It doesn't have to be an abundance or lack in material things, sometimes we have incredible joy from the love, attention and understanding we receive, or experience pain from the lack thereof. Sometimes the joy comes from the things we do and create that can be incredibly fulfilling and rewarding. The point is that if you are in a very low place in your life right now, don't worry, everything is going to be okay. Tomorrow will bring new opportunities with the rising of the sun. Just hang in there. It is just a season. There will be others which are better and some may even surprise you with unencumbered joy.

The thing about the low and difficult seasons is that you are at rock bottom. No way to go deeper. So the only way to go is up. The only direction that you can take will be an improvement in your condition. There is no lower. From here it is upwards. Just please remember that it is a season. That's it. You will see seasons in the complete opposite direction where you just can't feel more blessed or happy. Seriously. You will find yourself in the future in an extremely high season, you just need to get past all of this.

Also and on another subject, people will come in and out of your life. Some stay a brief time and some will be there for a long time. It hurts to see some people depart but there is always a reason under God. Some simply come into your life to teach you something and some are there to make you understand a lesson in life. Always cherish all of the people that come into your life and treasure the good ones. During the low seasons you will see the people that truly care about you rally around you and support you in those moments. These are the most important relations because they are there because they truly love you and not for some interest or convenience.

For me, I was able to use my low seasons for reading and edification. A big inspiration for me through these times was Joseph Campbell who relates his times of scarcity during the great depression where he would always find books to read. I would do the same. I would frequent the library and Barnes and Noble at every opportunity. Even though I was feeling horrible I was still able to lift a book and become incredibly interested in subjects, this time in psychology. I became enamored of this science and decided to attend a Masters program in clinical psychology. I learned a lot about myself and depression through this program and was able to lift myself out of this state only with the help and hand of God and my faith. It is not an easy thing to do. He showed me the way to life, understanding and freedom.

After that, I moved to New York City. My sister offered to have me live with her and I accepted the gracious invitation. I would live on 42nd and 9th street in the heart of Hell's kitchen. I would take jobs as a host in high end restaurants in Manhattan. For my commute I would walk up to 7th avenue and then take a cab heading north to 56th street. I would have to arrive at 5.30 am at the restaurant so I could get things in order and open the establishment. Some mornings were a big challenge because on 7th and 42nd where I grabbed my cabs there were always people who were still partying and ready to mug anyone in sight. Once again, the Lord always protected me. I came close to getting mugged at least three times but every time I was able to escape in the last fraction of a second. Unbelievable? Yeah, quite unbelievable but my Lord works miracles and He has always protected me and kept me safe. I never suffered any type of injury although I had crazy people coming at me with whatever they had in their hands at the time. Thank you Lord for so much. Thank you Lord for everything.

One fine day, my sister tells me that she needs to move to California and will I move with her. At first, I was hesitant but then I decided to ask random people on the street what they thought and every single one of them told me to go west. I did.

I moved with my sister to Foster City and then it was time to look for a job. It was here that I first started my career in marketing. Kerala Ayurveda was hiring for a part time admin job that was less than a mile away from where I was living. I put on my suit and went determined to get that job which then became full time admin and then director of Marketing. I worked with the Ayurvedic doctors and also learned a whole lot from them for five years. After that I freelanced my online marketing skills to many industries and made a decent living for myself. At this point is where I met a lady, fell in love and got engaged. It did not work out and she ended up kicking me out of her house. This marked for me my second lowest point in my life. My second large valley after being in so many high peaks in my life before. I fell into a depression but this was not as bad as the first one. I knew that with the help of God I could overcome it since I had already done so before so it was very different for me.

My point in telling you my story is to share my testimony. I tell you my life story, for you to see how the Lord has always cared for me, protected me, and taken care of all of my needs. I want to illustrate how the Lord has always been present in my life even when I was far away from Him. I am sharing my story with you because I want you to see how I built my faith throughout my life. I was not always the best Christian nor was I the best child of God. I was actually quite the opposite but the Lord had mercy and compassion on me. He had the utmost understanding and accepted me with all of my flaws and weaknesses. He will do the same for you. Just repent of your sins and turn towards the Lord. He will take care of everything else. Accept the Lord into your heart and your life will change. I promise you that.

Once again, I thank you for coming. I am grateful that you did. I wish in my heart that I could show you just how Miraculous and Beautiful this world is and what a gift it is to be alive. I wish I could show you just how Amazing Jesus is. But I can't. You have to see it for yourself. I could point you in the right direction and then you might make it a point to discover it.

Simply, I would say start by looking to the perfection and majesty of nature. Look upon these redwoods and sequoias, they all began as a set of miniscule seeds and look at what they have become. By the way, you can also do that – you can become anything you want to in this life. Miraculous, right?

Look upon the mason bee and the deep green sweat bee. They look to be designed by a sophisticated and modern design company or by a company like Tesla. Or look to the rest of the aesthetically stunning bees or dragon flies with their array and sharpness of bright colors. Beautiful, right? And what about the blue-green stealth hummingbirds. They maneuver very rapidly, have an excellent metabolism, and can travel distances of thousands of miles. Further, what if we consider the Homing pigeon. This messenger pigeon is miraculous in itself, it can travel very large distances and can find its nest without guidance, map or a gps. It can make it back home or to any starting point trough magnetoreception and can be trained to maneuver and turn sharply at speeds of up to 60mph. Today, people race them and they are well trained to avoid predatory hawks in their races which are typically distances of around 500+ miles.

And what about the full and crescent moons, the profound stars, the pink and purple skies at sunrise. The elongated dispersed clouds allowing rays of light to shine through. Just Gorgeous! Who paints a more beautiful picture but Our Lord. He is the creator and living sustainer of all of this magical, stunning and miraculous place. He paints the sky. He gives us the immense gift of life. A true and most precious gift. A gift more valuable than all of the gold, diamonds, and precious metals in the world. And If that wasn't enough He also promises us eternal life in his Kingdom if we follow his simple law and covenant. He give us Love and Understanding, He forgives our sins and gives us redemption. His love is never ending and always enduring. He listens to us when we speak to Him. He loves us unconditionally. He protects us, He covers us. He is our Lord and Savior. The Lord Jesus Christ.

And He gives us an opportunity in this life to become like a robust sequoia, like an imposing redwood tree. All we have to do is put in the work. Whether we grow strong physically, psychologically, mentally, or spiritually is entirely up to us. All of the potential is there. And He is waiting for you and waiting to listen to you. Pour your heart out to him, He will comfort you.

I wish I could show you just how beautiful you truly are. I wish I could show you just how incredibly unique and precious your soul is. I wish in my heart that I could teach you how to love yourself. But these are all things that you must discover and embark upon yourself. There is beauty in all living things but there is an extraordinary beauty in the individuality of things and You, my friend, are highly individual. There is not another person like you. There might be someone somewhere that looks kind of like you but they will have different personality traits, likes and dislikes, and temperament. In other words, it will be a different person altogether. You are highly unique. You are perfectly made and a beautiful soul who is more than worthy to be loved. No matter what you go through, no matter what people say or do to you, always remember this. You are beautiful. No one teaches us to love ourselves but it is essential in our growth and development to do so.

So I think that is enough for today. As you know, you are always welcome to come back at any time. My door is always open. We have much more to discuss and cover. Furthermore, once you come back we can learn different modalities of meditation, the science of breathing, self remembering, contemplation, and prayer. These are powerful tools for you. All of these practices are easy to learn and they will bring peace, grounding, and stability to your heart. We just need to get started.

Dear Lord, please forgive us our sins. Thank you for so many blessings and for always being by our side at all times. Thank you for saving, rescuing, hiding, and protecting me. Thank you Jesus. I am grateful for all of your abundant blessings. Thank you for this roof over my head, for running hot water and for our sustenance. Thank you Lord for being understanding, merciful and compassionate with us. I thank Thee for everything. For this heater that keeps me warm, for my family and friends and for my health and life. Thank you so much. I know that I cannot come close to repaying everything that you have done and continue to do for me. I understand that I can only hope to show you my appreciation with my love, devotion, following your law, abiding by your principles and by doing small acts in this world. I know that this is all you ask of us and that you truly do not ask for much, still, I hope to do it to the best of my capacity for all of the days of my life. I will forever hold on to your word, testimony, and example in my heart with the hope that I can one day dwell in your kingdom. I love you Jesus.

One thing I ask for the Lord, this only do I seek: that I may dwell in the house of the Lord, all the days of my life, to gaze on the beauty of the Lord and to seek Him in his temple.

Psalm27

In terms of those who claim that there is no proof of the existence of God I would simply say: I AM THE PROOF! My life and testimony is proof of the existence of God. If my life is not enough to prove My Lords existence then we can bring in many other lives and testimonies to prove it beyond the shadow of a doubt. In other words, if we were proving this in court or in any other setting we could begin with my testimony in Christ and then move on to other people's lives and testimonies. I assure you that there are hundreds of people who can also share their testimony.

Or we could begin with Jaime Perez. Mr. Perez is a baseball coach at his local high school in Edinburg, Texas. He was scheduled to have surgery in Houston for his battle with stage 3 cancer. His family, friends, and team came together to pray to our Lord for his recovery. Upon arriving for his procedure, the radiologists and doctors gave him the miraculous news that he was now completely cancer free. He rang the bell. He says that he wears his medical band to remind himself everyday of how the Lord healed him and provided him a second chance in life.

There are many others. My aunt is another testimony. She was diagnosed with thirty-two cancerous tumors by her doctors and was undergoing treatment. We all prayed for her. The Good Lord had compassion and mercy on her soul. She was given the news recently that she is now completely cancer free. The Lord, our God and Savior, Jesus Christ healed her. He saved her.

So my question to you is: how many testimonies would it take for you to be convinced beyond a reasonable doubt of the existence of our Lord? One hundred people and their testimonies? No Problem. One thousand testimonies? No problem at all. The Lord performs miracles in and for thousands of people. So what is stopping us from being able to say that there is more than enough proof for the existence of Our Lord? What would prohibit us from being able to affirm His existence? My answer is: Absolutely Nothing.

To be honest, I do not understand how people can say that there is no proof or evidence for the existence of God. That is simply not true. As you can see from my life, there is plenty of proof and evidence for the existence of God and plenty of eyewitnesses that can attest to the same. And it is not only my life testimony, I know many others who have experienced the same Love, Protection and Mercy from our Lord. You, I am sure, have seen at least some miracles in your lifetime.

Once again, I thank you for coming to see me. I will be praying for you. Prayer is very powerful and effective. Always remember that The Lord is always ready to listen.

Pro Tip: Be gentle with yourself. In other words, don't be too hard on yourself and try not to blame yourself for everything. We are always quick to blame ourselves for everything. That is not always the case. There are all types of factors, characters and circumstances that play into a situation. Furthermore, you are going through a difficult time right now so limit your expectations in regards to other issues. Don't try to take on too much. This is the time to dedicate to your healing and getting back up on your feet. Also, don't throw more problems into the mix to worry about or to be sad about. Don't do it. We have the tendency to pile up negative and destructive things when we are down on our emotions. Try to occupy your mind in creative and positive things. Also, we need to work on learning how to meditate. No matter what modality you choose it would be a good thing so that we can begin to take control of our thoughts and not be at their mercy. You are the captain of the ship. Enough for today. Let's wrap it up and we can continue in our next visit.

By way of summary, I would say that we come into this world directed at development, growth and advancement. Everywhere we see that the human being is pointed at improvement since inception. We grow to become more fully ourselves. We are here in this life to become the best version of ourselves. We can see improvements in our physical, mental, psychological, and spiritual beings if we put in the work and are disciplined and consistent in the same. The work is never finished as we can always become better in all aspects but improvement is always noticed.

As such, the goal is to work on ourselves to ultimately achieve the greatest perfection that we can as human beings. This we achieve by getting closer to God. The closer we get to God, the closer He draws to us. As you grow in your relationship with God you also grow in your love, capacities and understanding. This is the greatest perfection and attainment of the human being: to excel in becoming like a shining diamond through the spirit with a relationship with God.

Have mercy on me, O God,

According to your steadfast love;

According to your abundant mercy

Blot out my transgressions.

Wash me thoroughly from my iniquity,

And cleanse me from my sin.

Psalm 51

What is the meaning of life?

Does God exist?

AI:

The question of whether God exists or not is a deeply philosophical and subjective one, and opinions on this matter vary greatly among individuals and religious traditions. Some people believe in the existence of a higher power or deity, while others do not.

From a philosophical perspective, arguments for the existence of God include the cosmological argument, which posits that the universe must have had a cause, and that cause must have been God. The teleological argument states that the complexity and order of the universe suggest the existence of an intelligent designer. The moral argument asserts that objective moral values and duties cannot be grounded in naturalism and require a divine foundation.

On the other hand, arguments against the existence of God include the problem of evil, which questions how an all-powerful and all-loving God could allow evil and suffering to exist. The lack of empirical evidence for the existence of God is also a common objection.

Ultimately, whether or not God exists is a matter of personal belief and faith, and cannot be proven or disproven through objective scientific or philosophical inquiry.

ME:

No. This is not true. That God Exists can be proven and I have done so here by testimony. We also have many, many other testimonies that attest to that same fact: Our Lord Exists! Praise His Name!

There is more empirical evidence pointing to the existence of God than not. This world is light and dark. There is goodness on the one hand and there is evil on the other. This is the nature of the universe. The existence of evil has nothing to do with the existence or power of God. As we are reminded in the Holy Bible:

The light shines in the darkness, and the darkness has not overcome it.

John 1:5

What is the best way to live?
AI:

The meaning of life is a deeply philosophical and subjective question that has been debated by philosophers, theologians, and scientists for centuries. While there is no single, definitive answer to this question, many people believe that the meaning of life is to find happiness, purpose, and fulfillment through personal growth, relationships with others, and contributing to society in a meaningful way. Some people may find meaning through spirituality or religion, while others may find meaning through their work, hobbies, or relationships. Ultimately, the meaning of life is a deeply personal and subjective experience that can vary greatly from person to person.

ME:

The meaning of life is to foster growth, development and improvement to find happiness, purpose, and fulfilment. We must work at improving ourselves, including the greatest perfection which is to get closer to God, by getting closer to God you attain peace, love, and happiness. The Lord will also prosper you and show you His salvation. He will provide, protect, defend and cover you with His loving arms. What are you waiting for?

The best way to live is subjective and varies from person to person, as each individual has unique values, goals, and circumstances. However, there are some general principles that many people believe can lead to a fulfilling and meaningful life. Here are a few:

1. Cultivate positive relationships: Humans are social creatures, and cultivating strong, positive relationships with others can be a key factor in leading a happy and fulfilling life. This includes building close relationships with family and friends, as well as developing supportive networks in your community.

2. Pursue personal growth: Continuously learning, developing new skills, and seeking out new experiences can help you grow as a person and find meaning in life. This may involve setting and working

toward personal goals, trying new things, and seeking out new challenges.

3. Find a sense of purpose: Having a clear sense of purpose can help you stay motivated and focused on what matters most to you. This may involve pursuing a career or vocation that aligns with your values, or dedicating yourself to a cause or passion that you care deeply about.

4. Take care of your physical and mental health: Taking care of your physical and mental health is essential to living a fulfilling life. This may involve eating a healthy diet, getting enough sleep, exercising regularly, and seeking support when needed.

5. Practice gratitude: Gratitude involves taking time to appreciate the good things in your life, even amidst difficult times. Practicing gratitude regularly can help you maintain a positive outlook and find joy in everyday moments.

Ultimately, the best way to live is a deeply personal and subjective experience that depends on your unique values, circumstances, and goals.

ME:

Always begin your day by setting aside at least 5 minutes to thank God for everything that you have and practicing gratitude throughout your day. This practice will change your life.

Do we have free will?

AI:

The question of whether or not we have free will is a topic of much debate among philosophers and scientists. Free will is the concept that individuals have the ability to make choices that are not determined by prior causes or external factors.

Some argue that free will is an illusion, and that our actions and choices are determined by a complex set of factors, including genetics, upbringing, social and cultural influences, and environmental factors. According to this view, while we may feel that we are making free choices, our decisions are ultimately determined by a combination of these factors.

Others argue that we do have free will, and that our choices and actions are not entirely predetermined by external factors. According to this view, while our environment and circumstances may influence our choices, we still have the ability to make decisions that are not entirely determined by prior causes.

Ultimately, whether or not we have free will is a complex philosophical and scientific question, and opinions on this matter vary greatly. While it is possible that our choices and actions are determined by a combination of internal and external factors, many people still feel a sense of agency and control over their decisions and actions.

ME:

Yes. Absolutely, you have free will. You can choose the road of darkness or the road of the Light. It is all up to you. You choose your own adventure. Each road has a different outcome. Pro Tip: Choose our Lord, the light of this world and you will be delighted for He will fill your heart with gladness, peace and happiness.

My Go To Prayers

Our Father

Our Father, Who art in Heaven

Hallowed be Thy name

Thy Kingdom Come

Thy will be done

On earth as it is in heaven

Give us this day our daily bread

And forgive us our trespasses

As we forgive those who trespass against us

And lead us not into temptation

But deliver us from evil

Hail Mary

Hail Mary, full of grace

The Lord is with thee

Blessed art thou amongst women

And blessed is the fruit of thy womb, Jesus

Holy Mary

Mother of God

Pray for us sinners now and at the hour of our death

Amen

Glory be to the Father, and to the Son,

And to the Holy Spirit

Amen

My Favorite Bible Verses

When the righteous cry for help, the Lord hears

And delivers them out of all their troubles.

The Lord is near to the broken hearted

And saves the crushed in spirit.

Many are the afflictions of the righteous,

But the Lord delivers him out of them all.

Psalm 34

Through Him we have also obtained access by faith into this grace in which we stand

And we rejoice in hope of the glory of God

Not only that, but we rejoice in our sufferings,

Knowing that suffering produces endurance,

And endurance produces character,

And character produces hope,

And hope does not put us to shame,

Because God's love has been poured into our hearts

Through the Holy Spirit which has been given to us.

Romans 5

Be strong and courageous.

Do not fear or be in dread of them,

For it is the Lord your God who goes with you.

He will not leave you or forsake you.

Deuteronomy 31

Rejoice in hope, be patient in tribulation,

Be constant in prayer.

Romans 12

But they who wait for the Lord shall renew their strength

They shall mount up with wings like eagles

They shall run and not be weary

They shall walk and not faint.

Isaiah 40

And after you have suffered, the God of all grace,

Who has called you to his eternal glory in Christ,

Will Himself restore, confirm, strengthen, and establish you.

Peter 5

O Lord, you hear the desire of the afflicted;

You will strengthen their heart;

You will incline your ear

Psalm 10

For God gave us a spirit not of fear

But of power and love and self-control

Timothy 1

So that they should set their hope in God

And not forget the works of God,

But keep his commandments

Psalm 78

I love the Lord, because he has heard

my voice and my pleas for mercy.

Because he inclined his ear to me,

Therefore, I will call on him as long as I live.

The snares of death encompassed me;

The pangs of Sheol laid hold on me;

I suffered distress and anguish.

Then I called on the name of the Lord:

"O Lord, I pray, deliver my soul!"

Gracious is the Lord

And righteous

Our God is merciful.

The Lord preserves the simple;

When I was brought low, he saved me.

For you have delivered my soul from death,

my eyes from tears

my feet from stumbling

Psalm 116

You are a hiding place for me;

You preserve me from trouble;

You surround me with shouts of deliverance.

Psalm 32

He sent from on high, he took me;

He drew me out of many waters.

He rescued me from my strong enemy,

From those who hated me,

For they were too mighty for me.

They confronted me in the day of my calamity,

But the Lord was my support.

He brought me out into a broad place;

He rescued me, because he delighted in me.

Psalm 18

I sought the Lord, and He answered me
And delivered me from all my fears.
Psalm 34

For he deliver the needy when he calls,
The poor and him who has no helper.
He has pity on the weak and needy,
And saves the lives of the needy.
From oppression and violence he redeems their life,
And precious is their blood in his sight.
Psalm 72

Then they cried to the Lord in their trouble,
And He delivered them from their distress.
Psalm 107

Fear not, for I am with you
Be not dismayed, for I am your God
I will strengthen you, I will help you,
I will uphold you with my righteous right hand.
Isaiah 41

Made in the USA
Monee, IL
29 December 2023

50700780R00059